A PENNY

IN MY POCKET

To Reagan,
See a penny, pick it up!
Joyce Hill
5/17/11

A PENNY
IN MY POCKET

Joyce Hill

Mushgush Press

Johns Creek, GA

Photograph and cover design by Mushgush Press

For more information and activities relating to this book, go to www.apennyinmypocket.com

ISBN 978-0-9795818-1-6
ISBN 978-0-9795818-0-9 (hardcover)

Library of Congress Control Number: 2007941084

Published by Mushgush Press
335 Cantlegate Close, Johns Creek GA 30022

Printed in the U.S.A. 2007

Dedicated to:

Mom and Dad, who always told me,

"You should write a book."

Acknowledgments:

Heartfelt thanks go to my editor, Barbara Beattie. I must have found a lucky penny the day you came my way.

Thanks to the many teachers and friends who gave their "two cents' worth."

Thanks to my daughter Morgan, who so willingly read every chapter "hot off the press"; my son Max, for his ready wit (he'll "read it when it comes out on tape"); and above all, my husband William, who immigrated to this country, pursued the American dream and became my American dream husband.

CONTENTS   PAGE

1. THE PENNY DROPPED   1

2. A PENNY SAVED IS A
    PENNY EARNED: 1909   12

3. SEE A PENNY, PICK IT UP   37

4. PRETTY PENNY: 1918   47

5. IN FOR A PENNY,
    IN FOR A POUND   76

6. LUCKY PENNY: 1927   84

7. PENNIES FROM HEAVEN   112

8. A PENNY FOR YOUR
    THOUGHTS: 1933   124

9. COIN TOSS   151

10. TWO CENTS' WORTH: 1941   161

11. PRESENT YOUR PENNY
    DAY   177

    GLOSSARY OF PENNY
    EXPRESSIONS   195

    DISCUSSION QUESTIONS   199

A PENNY

IN MY POCKET

Chapter 1

THE PENNY DROPPED

Jay groaned as he lifted the heavy brown jug from the living room floor. How many years had his family been filling this enormous old thing with pennies? He set it awkwardly on the kitchen table and figured out the math. The jug had come with his family from India when they moved to the United States. He was only three when they moved; he really didn't remember it at all. Mom and Dad had told him that while they had been unpacking, he had raided Mom's purse. One by one, he had dropped her coins into the jug, like it was some sort of wishing well. He really had no idea what had been going through his mind. Maybe he wasn't happy about moving away from friends and was wishing to go back home to India. From then on, it had become a ritual to put pennies in the jug. He was twelve now, so that meant there were nine years' worth of pennies in the jug. No wonder it was so hard to lift.

He wrapped both arms around the jug and shook it at an angle to empty some pennies onto the table. He thought about why he needed the pennies and decided he may as well shake out a lot of them. Every now and then, a torrent of pennies would block the opening and Jay would have to upright the jug before he shook again, more slowly. Pennies covered the table, like a blanket of copper snow.

He heard the opening of the door that led from the garage into the kitchen. Mom was home from work. Wait—Mom was home! And he had covered the table in pennies!

"*Jaysukh*! What are you doing? I need to start dinner and you need to set the table soon. But, I don't see a table to set. You've made a mess!"

Mom was standing next to Jay with her hands on her hips. Whenever she said "*Jaysukh*," she meant business. She always seemed to have her hands on her hips when she said his full name. "Why did you empty the penny jug? And why now? On the kitchen table—before dinner?"

"Sorry. I forgot what time it was. It's for a social studies project. I need an old penny and figured there must be one in here."

"I'm sure you could have found an old penny without dumping so many out."

Jay spoke emphatically. "Well, I don't want just any old penny! I want the oldest penny. Everybody in class is doing this. Well," he paused, "maybe they're not all dumping them on the kitchen table, but they're all looking for old pennies."

Mom walked to the sink, washed her hands and began her usual activities of making dinner. The kitchen was filled with the familiar banging of cupboards and drawers being opened and shut, the clanking of pots as they were pulled out and set on the stove, and the sound of water running in the sink. She handed Jay the large pan that usually held chicken.

"You can clear the table by putting the pennies into this pan."

3

Jay thought it was time for a little comic relief, though Mom didn't always appreciate his jokes. "What's for dinner—*tandoori* pennies?"

"For *you*, maybe. No, I just thought you could clear up the table that way, but still be able to look through the pennies later." She seemed to have melted just a bit, like the delicious frozen *kulfi* she made if you didn't eat it fast enough.

"That's a good idea. When I look through them, I can put them into a bag. We could finally take them to that machine at the grocery store that sorts coins. I wonder how many we have!"

It took a number of swipes to clear the table of pennies. Jay was in the middle of setting the table when the garage door opened again and his little sister, Anju, ran into the kitchen. That meant that Dad and Raj were home, since they picked her up from the afterschool program. Raj took the high school bus to help Dad in the family's store after school. Mom and Dad didn't like whom he'd been hanging around with after school, so they had him spend his afternoons at the store. It wasn't long before they all sat down for dinner.

"How was school today, Jay? And you must answer with something other than your usual response." Dad asked the same question every night. And every night Jay said that it was boring.

"Jay, your father didn't see the kitchen table earlier. Why don't you tell us all about that?" Mom looked at him with a smile.

"Well, we have a project in Social Studies where we have to look for the oldest penny we can find. Then, we have to do a research report on that year. I kind of dumped out the jug full of pennies all over the kitchen table before dinner. Great timing 'cause Mom walked in just when I did it."

Jay was hungry and reached for some more rice. He poured some of the curry sauce from the chicken on it. He passed it to Raj who just shook his head. He noticed Raj wasn't paying any attention to anyone. That was typical lately.

"Ms. Maxwell said that we're supposed to find out what kids our age might've been doing that year. After we do our research we're supposed to hold the penny in our hand and think about a kid our age who may have held that exact same penny in their hand during that year."

5

Dad reached for a second helping as well. "That sounds better than the projects I did at school. I think my school days were much more boring than yours. Don't forget all that walking in snow ten miles to school, either."

"Dad, there wasn't snow in the part of India where you grew up. And, didn't you live across the street from the school?" Jay cocked his head and gave Dad his "give me a break" look.

"Oh, sorry. I guess that was a movie I saw." Dad winked at Anju, who giggled back at him.

"Jay had the good idea that we should finally cash in all those pennies we've saved. Why don't we come up with some kind of treat with the money?" Mom suggested.

Anju perked up at the word "treat." "A treat? Like candy or something?"

"Hey, Anju, we can get something a lot better than candy," Jay exclaimed. "There are tons of pennies."

"Can I help you look for an old penny? I want to help!"

6

Jay really wanted to look through the pennies himself. It would be so annoying if his pesky little sister found the oldest penny.

"It's my project. You can do your own little kid homework." That made Anju start to cry. How did she do that? Jumping with excitement one minute and turning on tears the next.

***

After the kitchen table was cleared of the remnants of dinner, Jay sat back down with the pan of pennies. He stared at them as he tried to come up with a method of searching through them. It was overwhelming, thinking of looking at every single penny in the pan. Plus, there were still so many more left in the jug. He decided to line up ten pennies, look at the dates and set aside the oldest one. Then, he'd take ten more pennies and look at them, comparing them to the oldest one from the last batch. He would just keep doing that. After thirty minutes, the oldest date he had was 1962 and Jay was getting tired of pennies. He was sure there must be some way that he could put Anju to work and still get credit for the oldest penny. And get credit for being a nicer big brother than he really was.

He told Anju that once he came up with the oldest penny out of each group of ten, she could gather up the remainder and put them in a tote bag. That would save some time. He tried to hide his shock when Raj walked up to the table.

"I guess it's a good thing they didn't do this project when I was in your grade. I would've gone through that jug of pennies already," he said, with what Jay thought might even be a hint of a smile.

Jay was happy that Raj wasn't being surly, as Mom called it, and wanted to keep him talking. He missed doing fun stuff with him. They used to go outside and explore the woods together after school. He wondered if their old fort was still there. He decided he didn't care about the glory of finding the old penny himself.

"I could use some more help. I'm going crazy. Could you help me for a few minutes?"

Raj shrugged his shoulders, but sat down at the table. "What's the oldest one you found so far?"

"I've got one from 1962, but I still have lots of pennies. I really want to find the oldest one in my class. I bet nobody has more pennies to look through. I've been looking at them ten at a time, pulling out the oldest then comparing that to the next ten. It seems to be working pretty well." Jay talked quickly, as if he were afraid if he took too long, Raj would leave.

Raj didn't say anything, but Jay watched him take a handful of pennies from the pan and count out ten. Jay heard his mother's light footsteps come to the kitchen door, then quickly turn around and leave. He thought she probably couldn't believe that the three kids were quietly doing something together and that she didn't want to ruin the rare moment. He thought about making a joke about it aloud to Raj, but he didn't want to ruin the moment either. These days, you had to be careful around him; you never knew how he was going to act. Raj and Anju seemed to have that trait in common, lately.

"Hey! What's this doing in here?" Raj was holding up a small silver coin. "It's a rupee! I remember these from when we went on that trip to India last year."

Anju looked at the coin and got a sheepish look on her face. "I put that in there. Mommy bought me that silk coin purse when we were in India. When we got home and I found out I couldn't use the leftover money here, I got mad and dumped it in the jug."

"Hey, that's okay. The whole jug of pennies started getting filled when I dumped coins in it!" Jay laughed.

The three of them returned to the task of sorting the pennies. "Raj, can you tell what this says? It's so worn and dirty I can't read it. Maybe that means it's really old."

Raj picked up the penny and turned it back and forth. "I can't read it either, but I have an idea. Did you ever do that science experiment that cleaned pennies? I did it as a kid but we just talked about it again in Chemistry."

"Wait a minute—doesn't it use salt or something?"

"It's salt and vinegar. You'll like this, Anju!"

Anju beamed at being included in her brothers' activity. Jay went to the cupboard to get out the salt while Raj went to the pantry to look for vinegar. He came back with the vinegar, a small bowl and a paper towel. Anju excitedly got on her knees on the chair to get a better view.

Raj mixed the salt and vinegar in the bowl. "Go ahead and put the penny in. The acid should remove the oxidation from the penny. That penny is really a mess, so let it sit in there a bit. Then rub it with the paper towel."

Jay dropped the penny in the grainy, cloudy mixture. Raj made them laugh as he hummed the theme from Jeopardy while they waited.

"Is it ready yet? Can you tell?" Anju wiggled with impatience.

"Let's find out. Come on Jay, wipe it off and let's see!"

Jay lifted the penny out from the bowl and wrapped the paper towel around it, without looking. He rubbed and rubbed, and then he pulled the penny out of the paper towel.

It still looked well-used and well-traveled, but it was clean enough for the date to be read. An incredulous look spread across Jay's face. There, in his hand was a penny from 1909.

Chapter 2

A PENNY SAVED IS A PENNY EARNED

Nick tried not to breathe in as he sat on the front porch using his rusty boot scraper on his shoes. He hurriedly wiped the filth of the Chicago streets from the soles. He had just returned from helping Papa at the fruit and vegetable stand. Peddlers with horse-drawn carts shared the unpaved roads with pedestrians, stray animals, streetcars and the occasional Model T. Back home in Greece, Nick used to run around barefoot most of the time. That would never work on the streets of Chicago in 1909.

Nick thought of how sick he was of all the bad smells. The hot summer sun had been simmering the garbage, manure and stockyard smells into some kind of putrid soup. He couldn't imagine working in the meat-packing plants like so many of the other new Chicago immigrants. He'd probably never eat meat again.

Once his shoes were as clean as he could get them, he went into the house where he, Papa and his brother Alex lived with eight other men and boys. He set the shoes by the inside of the door next to another worn pair of shoes. The fragrant aroma of *moussaka* was a welcome relief to the rancid smells outside. He knew it had been made with the eggplants he'd brought home from the stand the day before. They'd been too soft to sell to customers, but were good enough for them. It wasn't quite Mama's cooking, but he was sure that he ate better than other boys and men who shared living quarters. Whenever Jane Addams, the lady who ran Hull House, came by to check on things, she always commented on the good conditions in their quarters. She said the Greek men ran a clean, well-fed household while they waited for their wives to come over from Greece. She talked about the many groups of men who lived in conditions like that of a pigsty. This gave Papa and the other men all the more reason to boast of their Greek upbringing.

13

"*Yahsu, Theodorus!*" Nick said to an older man who was taking a heavy-looking pan off the cast-iron stove.

"*Yahsu, Nikolaos!* I mean to say 'Hello, Nick.' You teach me English. I don't teach Greek to you," the man firmly stated in a heavy accent.

"Okay, Theo," responded Nick.

Theo look puzzled. "Why you speak Greek again and say 'no' to me?"

"Remember, I told you that 'okay' means yes in English. It sounds like *ohee*, the Greek word for no. And the word 'no' in English sounds like *neh*, the Greek word for yes. It's very confusing," explained Nick. "You'll learn in time."

"When I shop at Greek stores, I can still say *ohee* and *neh*! With you, I say 'okay' and 'no,' okay?" Theo flashed his warm, wide smile.

"Okay! Papa asked me to come home to help you while he and Alex close the fruit stand. What can I do?"

"I understand English better than I speak it. Set the table, please. Wash your hands first, *parakaloh*—I mean, please," instructed Theo.

As Nick got out the plates, utensils and glasses, he thought how he wouldn't be living in this house of men much longer. He'd miss them; they'd become like family. But soon, his real family would be together again. The thought of seeing Mama and Helen again filled him with an anticipation that almost hurt. After two years of being apart, they would be boarding a steamship from Greece the next day. In two weeks they would arrive in Chicago. Then his family would live together in their own rented house.

"*Nikolaos*! I mean, Nick," called out Theo. "Soon you will be English teacher for your mother and sister, Helen, right?"

"I can't wait. Papa told my brother and me that we need to buy them each a present. I was thinking of books for learning English. At least everybody in the neighborhood speaks Greek, so they can shop and meet people as soon as they get here."

They were interrupted by the front door opening and the boisterous sounds of men singing an old sailing song in Greek, followed by laughter. Nick realized it wouldn't be so lively once he was living with Mama and Helen. At least he could still hang out at the boy's club at Hull House—that was always a lot of fun. They had two lanes for bowling as well as billiard tables for the boys to use. There weren't just Greek boys there but immigrants from many countries, including Ireland, Russia, Poland and Italy. His best friend was *Pietrik*, who had come with his family from Poland.

"*Yahsu*, men!" greeted one of the group. The older men spoke more Greek than the younger ones. They often mixed English and Greek words together in the same sentence.

Soon, the four singers were joined by Papa, Alex and two brothers in their twenties who lived with them. The older brothers hadn't been in America for very long and didn't speak much English.

"*Pee-nao!*" Papa announced, boisterously. "I'm hungry! Do I smell *moussaka*?"

"Yes, Papa. Everything is ready. I set the table already."

At the dinner table, the older men engaged in deep conversation in Greek. Nick could tell they were talking Greek politics. The men were discussing things they had read in the Chicago Greek newspaper, *The Hellas*. Often they sat around the

16

Café Appolyn, drinking coffee and sharing Greek news. They may live here, thought Nick, but their hearts are still in Greece. He turned to Alex to talk about things closer to their new home.

"Are you ready for the wrestling match at Hull House this weekend?"

"Of course." Then Alex lowered his voice to a whisper. "Are you going to bet on me?"

Nick lowered his voice to match Alex's whisper. "I've never bet before, Alex. I don't have enough money. I've been saving for a present for Mama and Helen. I can't lose any of my money."

"Lose?" Alex's voice boomed. He looked around at the rest of the men at the table, and then lowered his voice again. "What do you mean, lose? Are you saying I'm gonna lose? That better not be what you mean. I'm a sure thing, little brother. You could get Mama and Helen something very special if you bet your money on me."

Nick felt trapped. He knew Alex hung around with some boys that got in trouble. They lived in crowded apartments with groups of other boys. Some of them had already quit school and were working in the meat-packing plants. That's why

Papa encouraged the boys to spend their spare time at Hull House, with all of its activities.

"I believe in you. I didn't mean that. I just don't have much money. I wouldn't feel right gambling with money meant for a present for Mama and Helen. I only have the pocket money from helping at the fruit stand. I *know* you'll win."

"Well then, as they say in America, why don't you put your money where your mouth is?" taunted Alex.

Nick was starting to feel as sick as he did when he smelled the Chicago Stock Yards, with their animals and butchered meat. Alex had been acting different lately and it scared Nick.

Their conversation was interrupted by Papa. He began, in his heavy Greek accent, "Sons, I found out something interesting today. There is a brand new 1909 penny. It has President Lincoln's picture on it. It's been made to mark one hundred years since Abraham Lincoln was born. I got some of the pennies when people bought fruit today. I set two aside—one for each of you. Here they are." He pushed them down the table toward his sons.

"Thanks, Papa," each of the boys said. Papa then returned to his conversation with the other men.

"That's a sign," Alex whispered to Nick. "If you bet on me, the money is going to come in as easy as you just got that penny."

Papa stood up and spoke in his native Greek. "I have a lecture that I want to attend tonight at Hull House. It is about the achievements of the classical period. It's going to be done in Greek and English. Alex, it is your turn to clean up the dishes with Philip."

"I can walk with you to Hull House, Papa," said Nick, in English. Although he understood all of the Greek, he was finding it easier to talk in English these days. "I signed up for some dark room time for my photography class. I'm going to develop some photographs I took." He stood up. "*Theodorus, escareefso*—the *moussaka* was delicious. Thank you!"

It was nice to have time alone with Papa as they walked to Hull House. There were always so many other people around that they hardly got a chance to talk to each other.

"Maybe you can take pictures of your mama and sister when they arrive. Helen must have grown so much in these two years. My little girl will be eight years old soon. And my lovely Sophia." Papa let out a deep sigh. "Their names are perfect for them. Helen is beautiful. Your mama is too, but she is a very wise woman, like her name says. As hard as we all have worked these two years, it has also been very hard on your mother. She has patiently waited until we felt we could send for her and Helen."

Nick wanted to talk to Papa about Alex's gambling suggestion, but feared his brother's backlash at him. He missed the days when he and Alex were close. Maybe things would get better once Mama arrived.

"*Nikolaos*, we will be busy in the next couple weeks before Mama and Helen get here. We need to get settled in the new house. We also have to finish getting the new ice cream shop ready. Next week, the fruit stand will be sold and we'll move up to our ice cream shop. Are you ready?"

"I can't wait, Papa. I'm tired of fruit all the time. I'd much rather eat ice cream." Nick patted his stomach dramatically.

"You may not believe it now, but just as you're tired of fruit, you'll be tired of ice cream. But it will be a fun place to work. Getting ice cream is always a happy time. Maybe you can take a picture of the ice cream store on opening day. Maybe your picture could get into *The Hellas*. That would be good advertising."

"You're a good businessman, Papa."

"Thank you, *Nikolaos*. I am very careful with money. I try to save and spend wisely. I don't even like to waste a penny. I hope you learn that from me. Even that one Lincoln penny I gave you is important. It's the pennies that add up. When you're smart with money, your pennies grow into dollars."

That made Nick think again about the wrestling bet Alex wanted him to make. He knew that wasn't the way to make money. Boys would brag about money they won, but he knew they never talked about all of their losses. He just had to figure out how to get out of it without getting Alex mad.

The two of them arrived at Hull House. Nick was always amazed at the activity that went on there every night. He heard that there were as many as five hundred boys there in an evening. The gymnasium and the basement recreation room with the bowling alleys and billiard tables were always crowded. But there was also a study room and library with a thousand books. There were evening classes of all types held, with a history room, chemistry lab and more. Some boys, who had no homes, lived in the Culver Club on the third and fourth floors. There were adult residents who lived there as supervisors. Many volunteers resided there as well. The nursery and kindergarten for children of working parents were an important part of the immigrant community.

Papa went into Bowen Hall, an auditorium that seated 750 people. Nick went up to the second floor where the dark room was located. In the calm of the dark room, Nick felt at peace. He loved the process of developing images onto paper. It thrilled him every time a picture came to life. As he watched the chemical solution work its magic on the paper, Nick felt it work its magic on him as well. His conversation with Papa had given him an idea that might get him out of his gambling dilemma. He'd ask the photography instructor if he'd be able to borrow a camera for the wrestling match on Saturday. He would be too busy taking pictures from the side of the gym to get approached about placing a bet. Nick would tell Alex that he was planning on taking a picture of his wrestling win. He would try to get it published in *The Hellas.* Alex wouldn't be mad at him if he could get his picture in the newspaper. Nick felt a wave of relief wash over him.

He clipped his pictures up to dry, airing them like clothes on the wash line back at the house. He then looked for his photography instructor. He found him at a desk, looking at some students' photographs.

"Excuse me, Mr. Wilson. I have a favor to ask. I was wondering if I could borrow a camera on Saturday to take photographs of the wrestling match. I want to try and get one published in the Greek newspaper, *The Hellas.*"

"Nick, that's a great idea. The wrestlers are all from the Greek community. I'd think the newspaper would like to publish a picture. Stop by Saturday afternoon and I'll be here to sign a camera out to you. You really like photography, don't you?"

"I do. I feel like a magician when I take a picture and develop it."

"That's just how I feel about it, Nick. I hope you stick with it."

"I hope so too. I'd like to save up and buy my own camera one day. First, I'm saving to buy a present for my mother and sister. They're coming from Greece soon. We'll be moving into our own house then."

"I have an idea for a present for them, Nick. It shouldn't be expensive at all, and I'm sure it will mean a lot to them. Why don't you take some pictures with one of our cameras? I'm sure someone in the carpentry shop here would make frames for you for at a very small cost. That would give your mother and sister something to hang up at the new house. What do you think?"

"I like that! I'll think of something they'll each really like a picture of. I was going to get them a book for learning English, but I like this idea better. There are plenty of books at the library here they can use. Thank you, Mr. Wilson!"

***

The next day Papa had to take care of some business at the new ice cream parlor. For one thing, the new sign was going up. Many a night at the supper table had been spent trying to figure out the perfect name for the store. He wanted a name that let the community know it was Greek-owned. But Papa said that he was raising an American family, in the land of opportunity, and didn't want the name to be *too* Greek. The Greek alphabet was totally different from English, so he didn't want to put any Greek letters on the sign. When Papa had announced his final decision for the name, the whole table of men had applauded.

"YaYa's Ice Cream! Spelled out y-a-y-a." It was perfect. Pronouncing the English spelling sounded just like the Greek word for grandmother. Any Greek person who said the name would realize they were saying Grandma, with all the associations of being spoiled by good food. Non-Greeks would just think "YaYa" was a fun name.

While Papa arranged for the new sign to be installed, Nick and Alex were left in charge of the fruit stand. As soon as there was a lull in the customers, Alex posed the question that Nick had been dreading.

"So, little brother. The big wrestling match is day after tomorrow. Are you for me, or against me, if you know what I mean?" Alex narrowed his eyes as he asked the question.

Nick avoided the betting implication made by Alex. He hoped to play on his brother's big ego and steered the subject to his plan.

"I'm *for* you, Alex. I think you're the best wrestler in Chicago."

"Now, you're talking."

"I got permission to borrow a camera from Hull House to take pictures at the match. I'm going to work hard at getting great shots of you pinning your opponents. I'll submit the best one to *The Hellas*. I'm betting they'll put a picture of the winner on the front page." He felt like his heart had just stopped. Why did he use the word betting? That was probably the only thing Alex had heard. He felt his face get warm as he waited for Alex's response.

"The front page! That'll really impress the girls. Do you think you can?"

Nick allowed himself to relax a bit. "I know I can take a good photograph but you need to win the match for the newspaper to want to publish it."

***

On Saturday, Papa let Nick off for the afternoon to pick up the camera and start taking photographs for his gifts. As he walked out the front door of Hull House, he felt like he was walking on air. A brand new Brownie camera had just been donated. The staff had practiced using it, but Nick was the first student they were allowing to experiment with it. As he walked down the street, carrying the box by its handle, he imagined he was a professional photographer on his way to take important pictures.

He stood on the side of the street and looked back at the mansion that was Hull House. He closed his left eye and framed the image with his thumb and forefinger. He visualized taking a photograph of the building.

"People are going to start saying strange things about you if you keep doing that. Well, stranger than what they already say."

Nick turned and saw his friend, *Pietrik*, with his blond hair and blue eyes—such a sharp contrast to his own dark features.

"Hi, *Pietrik*. Oh, sorry, I forgot you decided to call yourself Peter. I don't care what people think. I have important photographs to take today. Look at this new camera!"

"That black box you're carrying is a camera?"

"Yeah, look at this."

Nick squatted down and rested the black box on his knees. He unfastened the front latch, unhooked the hinges on each side and stretched out the pleated neck of the lens.

"That looks like the accordion my father plays all his Polish polkas on."

"The accordion thing is what makes it fold up. It's called the Folding Pocket Brownie."

"Who'd you steal it from?"

"Very funny. I checked it out from Hull House. I'm going to take some pictures to frame as gifts for my mother and sister."

"I'm heading there to go bowling now. Don't you want to come?"

"Nah, I'm going to take the pictures."

"Hey, take one of me. Your sister can have a photograph of me on her nightstand. The last face she'd see each night." Peter posed with a foolish grin on his face.

"I don't want her having nightmares as soon as she gets here. See you later."

Nick knew of a house with a garden full of flowers. This was where he would take the photograph for Helen. He knelt down on the sidewalk in order to get the angle of flowers against the sky. It was disappointing to know that the beautiful pinks, purples and deep blue sky that he was seeing would only be shades of black and white in the photograph. He tried to focus on the different heights and textures to make up for the lack of color.

For Mama, Nick wanted to find a setting that would make her know that there were nice places in Chicago. He knew she'd be homesick for awhile. He remembered how awful he felt when he first moved to Chicago. He had missed Mama so much. At least she'd have the whole family together. The first few days after he had arrived, everything had been new and exciting. After that, everything felt strange and ugly. In time, as he made friends and

29

was busy, there were more and more days he could even say he was happy. He knew that Mama and Helen would go through all those feelings too.

Nick had an idea. He'd take a picture for Mama of something important from their new life in America. He hurried to the family's fruit stand where Papa was weighing some cherries for a woman. Alex was rearranging the fruit to fill in blank spaces.

"Alex, will you cover the stand for a few minutes? I need Papa for a photograph."

"I guess I'd better stay on your good side until that picture gets in the papers. As long as Papa says it's okay. Don't forget, I get Monday afternoon off since you got today."

When Papa finished his sale with the woman, Nick told him his plan. Papa agreed as long as it didn't take too long. As the two of them walked down the street, Nick told Papa about the Brownie camera. They reached their destination and as they stopped on the sidewalk, Nick explained how the camera worked.

"Where should I stand? Do you want me to smile?"

"Just a minute." Nick stepped back and looked into the viewfinder. "Take a couple steps to the left. And give a big smile. Remember, you're smiling for Mama."

The scene which Nick saw for just a brief moment through the viewfinder was one he would see for years, hanging on the wall of his family's living room: Papa, with a big smile, meant just for Mama, standing outside YaYa's Ice Cream.

***

The gymnasium was packed that night for the wrestling match. Friends and family lined the walls around the floor. Nick pushed his hair out of his eyes and wiped the sweat from his forehead onto his pants. He kept glancing around for Alex's gambling buddies. Nick had purposely not put any money in his pocket so he could honestly say that he couldn't place a bet. Whenever anyone looked his way, he busied himself with the camera. He had adjusted and readjusted the settings as he tried to appear too occupied to be interrupted. To anyone watching, the simple-to-use camera must have seemed like a very complex apparatus.

"Hey, Alex's little brother. What ya got there?"

Nick tried to keep a steady voice. He'd seen this kid around his brother. Something about him seemed slippery, like if there was trouble around he'd just slide on out of sight.

"It's a camera. I'm taking photographs of the match."

"I got all my money on your brother, kid. How much did you put on him?"

"I can't place a bet. My pockets are empty." Nick thought his line sounded too rehearsed. An eel. This kid was a slick eel. He looked over at Slick for a reaction.

"Empty? What squirt kid's pockets are empty? They're usually full of junk. Come on, kid. Empty 'em out. Show me what you got."

Nick held onto the camera with his right hand and with his left, pulled his left pocket inside out. It was empty.

"Other one."

Nick switched hands and pulled out his right pocket. Something clinked to the floor. He looked down and saw Lincoln's face on the new penny Papa had given him to save. He had never taken it out of his pocket the other night.

"Empty, huh?"

As Slick bent over to pick up the penny, Nick wondered if there was any chance that it would slide right out of his slippery hands.

"What have we got here? Ooh—a new penny. Looks like you have something to bet with alright."

Nick did some fast thinking. "Listen, we both know Alex is going to win the match. But my father gave me that penny to keep. I'll be in big trouble if I lose it. How about if I keep the penny in my pocket? If for some reason Alex loses, then I'll give you a different penny from home. If he wins, you don't even have to give me anything else. Fair?" Nick felt like he was getting slippery. Maybe Slick was like a Model T and had sprung an oil leak that had oozed onto him.

"Here's your precious penny. I'm outta here. Go take some pictures."

Nick figured Slick had gotten tired of hanging out with small change and had gone on to find fuller pockets. He finally relaxed and gave his full attention to the gymnasium floor.

He saw Alex standing on the side, waiting to get on the mat next. Alex caught Nick looking at him and starting posing and hamming it up for the camera. Nick smiled and pretended to click away. That was the brother he remembered; maybe there was still hope for him.

It was a long evening of some intense wrestling. There were lots of Greek boys who were experienced wrestlers; all of them were expecting to win. By the end of the match, Nick had some great pictures of his brother. He was thrilled when Alex was declared the winner of the evening's matches. He knew his reasons were selfish ones: he had weaseled himself out of getting involved with gambling, his brother would be much easier to live with, and there was a chance he'd get a photograph in the newspaper.

By Monday morning, Nick had developed and dried his photographs. He took the best one of his brother to the offices of *The Hellas* newspaper. The editor was impressed with his work and said he'd try to find a spot for the picture in the paper. He couldn't promise anything, but told Nick to keep his eye on the newspaper. Nick was pretty sure that Alex would take care of that all by himself.

While Alex had been gloating a bit about his win, something else seemed a little different about him. Nick asked him the name of the guy who had made him empty his pockets, so that he could think of him by his real name. Alex said his name was Frank, but since he was such a smooth operator everyone called him Slick. Nick bit his lip to keep from laughing.

Alex spoke in a nicer voice than he had in a long time. "I learned something about those guys Saturday night. I don't think they're real friends. I was just a means to an end for them, a way to line their pockets. Those guys are losers. Wrestling at Hull House is fine, but I think I'm going to join the high school wrestling team. It might be a chance to meet some new guys."

"Mama will be real proud of you when she comes."

"That's what I want. That, and to meet some of the girls that hang out with the high school wrestlers," Alex laughed.

Nick reached his hand into his pocket and felt the penny Papa had given him. He felt rich.

Chapter 3

SEE A PENNY, PICK IT UP

Amelia had an idea. She always seemed to have an idea. The problem was they were the kind of ideas that ended up getting her into trouble. Not serious trouble, but as her friend Katherine called it, Lucy and Ethel trouble. Amelia and Katherine loved to watch old reruns of *I Love Lucy*, laughing and cringing at the same time, while Lucy dragged Ethel into yet another scheme bound to go bad. The ideas always seemed so good at the beginning. Just like this one did.

She needed to find an old penny for a school project. But there weren't many pennies in the house. Mom worked at a bank and as soon as there were fifty pennies, she'd roll them in a penny wrapper. When she had two rolled wrappers, then she'd take them to the bank to exchange for a dollar bill. Luckily, there had been one roll of pennies in the kitchen drawer. Mom said she could open it back up and look through them for an old penny. She gave Amelia a good tip. She said that old pennies had a picture of wheat on the back, not the Lincoln Memorial. But not a single penny in the roll had wheat on the back of it. The oldest penny had been from 1971. Amelia loved competition, and she wanted an older penny than that.

That's when she got the idea. She could almost see the flash from the light bulb above her head when the thought came to her. She knew a place that probably had more pennies than anywhere else in town. And if she got to it first, then she'd have her pick of all the pennies. If she found a penny she wanted, she'd just replace it with a nickel. There couldn't be anything wrong with that.

Since she was a little girl she'd been throwing pennies and making wishes into the fountain next to City Hall. Everyone she knew had done that. Think of all the pennies that must be in there! Maybe somebody cleared it out now and then, but every time she'd been there the bottom of the fountain was filled with pennies. But it would be a lot more fun with someone else. She'd call Katherine.

Katherine wasn't in her class, so she didn't have to do the penny project. But she was always up for an adventure. Well, with just a little pressure.

"Hey Katherine, it's Amelia. I have an idea!"

There was an exaggerated moan on the other end of the line. "Oh no, that dreaded word again. Another idea!"

"Wait, you have to listen to this. It'll really be fun. Remember that penny project I told you I had to do for Social Studies?" Amelia explained her idea of trying to find an old penny in the fountain. As usual, Katherine was skeptical.

"That's someone's wish you'd be taking out. What if you cause their wish to not come true?"

"I don't even know if throwing a coin and making a wish even works. Mine never came true. Even if it did work, do you think the penny has to stay in there forever for it to come true? I would think it's the throwing of the penny and making the wish that's the important part. They must clear the fountain out sometimes and give the money to charity or something. So those pennies are taken out."

"Giving it to charity probably helps the wish. I think you're messing with fate or something. Maybe it's even illegal."

"I didn't know you were so superstitious. I don't want to mess with fate or get arrested over a social studies project. If I take out a penny I'll replace it with something bigger. Maybe that increases the chances of the wish coming true; did you ever think of that? I'll go in to City Hall and tell them my plan and see what they say. If they say it's okay, then will you help me?"

"I'll go with you if they say it's okay, but I'm not keeping anyone's wish."

***

Amelia stopped and looked into the fountain on her way to City Hall. It was loaded with coins and most of them were pennies. It was a veritable treasure chest for her social studies project. Veritable. Amelia had just learned that the word meant "true" or "absolute" and found it a very handy word to know. She liked the sound of it and was thinking it or using it every chance she got. Katherine was a veritable worrywart. She had reminded Amelia of the saying, "You can't fight City Hall," trying to convince her that it wasn't worth asking if she could look for a penny in the fountain. Well, no harm in trying. Amelia was a veritable optimist.

She climbed the steps and pulled open the heavy doors of the brick building. This was one of the oldest buildings in town and very impressive. She tried not to be intimidated. She walked up to the woman at the help desk and explained her idea. Amelia thought that if the woman worked at something called a "help" desk, then she should certainly find a way to help Amelia get the pennies. She nervously brushed her auburn hair behind her ears.

The woman smiled at her. "I think I can help you." Amelia wondered if the woman had to say that since she worked at the help desk.

"We do have a law that says there's no bathing in the fountain. But we once researched how it was handled in Rome when people took coins out of Trevi fountain. The Italians decided that it's no more illegal to take the coins out than it is to put them in. But they didn't want to stop people from putting coins in since they raise a lot of money for charity from all the tourists throwing in coins. But they've also caught people taking coins from the fountain to keep. They have the same law we do against bathing in the fountain, so that's the law they use to arrest the people. But if you were to sit on the side of our fountain and check the pennies within your reach, I don't see any problem. Especially if you replace one you take with a larger coin. Wait a minute, there's the mayor. Let's ask her opinion!"

Amelia didn't really want to talk to the mayor. She liked the answer from the help desk lady just fine. She thought of what Mom always said, though—you catch more flies with honey than vinegar. She stood up tall, remembered to stop playing with her hair, and gave the mayor a big smile.

The helpful woman began, "Ms. Mayor, this young lady has an interesting question. We'd like to get your opinion on it."

Amelia again explained her idea for looking for an old penny in the fountain. She tried to be her most persuasive self. She hoped the mayor wasn't a veritable grouch.

The mayor was quiet for a moment as she appeared to think through the fountain issue. Then her face lit up. "I have an idea!"

A kindred spirit! Without even hearing the idea, Amelia decided that the town was very lucky to have this woman as mayor. A woman with ideas. Her kind of woman.

"We are way overdue in clearing the coins from the fountain. Our maintenance department is responsible for that, but they've been too busy to see to it. We can lend you a pair of boots and buckets, and you can take out all of the coins. You can look through the pennies as you do it. We'll let you choose which charity in town gets the money this time. How does that sound?"

Amelia felt like she'd been backed right into a corner, like an animal with no way to escape. This was one smart mayor. Amelia would get to look for pennies like she wanted and the mayor would get a big chore done, without her employees having to do it. Amelia could choose the charity, so she'd look bad if she didn't agree. She had no choice.

"May I have a friend help me?"

"Sure, we have plenty of boots."

***

The following Saturday morning, Amelia and Katherine were sloshing through the fountain, in men's large, black, rubber boots, hoping no one from school saw them.

Katherine muttered as she dredged for coins. "I keep tripping in these gargantuan galoshes. So help me, if I fall in . . ."

"You are the best friend anyone could have. Better even than Ethel. Wait, I have an idea!"

"Nooooooo!" wailed Katherine.

"This is a good thing. Since I dragged you into this, you can pick the charity the money goes to. How about that?"

"Now, that's a good idea. I've been thinking about where the money should go. What about the soup kitchen? I've helped serve the food to the needy there before. I know it would help them a lot."

Amelia laughed. "We're both just full of good ideas!"

They set to work looking at pennies, comparing dates and setting old ones on the side of the fountain. Two buckets had as many coins in them as they could lift. They were starting to fill a third bucket. Their hands were getting numb from the cold fountain water.

Katherine rubbed her hands together to warm them up. "I don't think they have to worry about anyone taking a bath in this water. Brrrr . . ."

Amelia looked around the fountain. "I have another idea. Maybe some people threw too high and their coins landed on top of that column, where the water sprays out when the fountain is turned on. There's a flat part up there. Coins could have been hidden up there for years."

She plodded to the center of the fountain. She stood on her tip toes and reached up to feel the ledge of the column. She could feel the edge of a coin up there. As she stretched a bit more and could just reach it, she heard a strange gurgling noise. By the time she figured out what it was, it was too late. She later referred to it as a veritable geyser and said memories of a trip to Old Faithful flooded over her. Through the sound of water rushing down on her head she could hear Katherine laughing hysterically. Amelia heard something that sounded like, "Do you have any ideas now?" but it was hard to be sure with Niagara Falls pounding in her ears.

Her boots were filled with water, and she trudged clumsily over to the edge of the fountain. With water still pouring off her, she sat down, next to a doubled-over Katherine.

"That was the funniest thing I've ever seen!" Katherine spurted out through her convulsive laughter. "I wish I could've filmed that!"

"I'm glad you enjoyed it. I guess it wasn't one of my better ideas." Amelia looked down at the coin she'd picked up and then grabbed and shook Katherine's sleeve with her other hand.

"Look! It was worth every drop of water. Look when it's from!"

In her hand, she held a veritable penny from the year 1918.

Chapter 4

PRETTY PENNY

Penny—Penelope when she was in trouble—sat on the cushioned window seat in her bedroom, staring out at the cobblestoned streets of Philadelphia. Her knees were drawn up to her chest, with her arms wrapped around the pinafore of her dress. She unclasped her arms and started twisting her copper-colored hair around and around an ink-stained finger—a nervous habit, which despite regular reminders, her mother couldn't break. Penny was a fidgety girl, even on a normal day. This wasn't a normal day, though. Today wasn't normal because of tomorrow. Tomorrow was her birthday. To top things off, school had been canceled.

School wasn't being canceled just for tomorrow, but indefinitely, which held the delicious possibility of forever. She knew in her head that it wouldn't be forever, but indefinitely was the next best thing.

Maybe the ink stains on her fingers would get a chance to fade away, since she wouldn't have to deal with the messy inkwell all day at school.

The reason school was being canceled, though, was so awful that it took away some of the sweetness. Penny thought it was as if someone gave you the most amazing piece of chocolate, but a little while after popping it in your mouth you found out it wasn't a normal piece of chocolate. It had some kind of mysterious property that made it, every now and then, taste like brussels sprouts. Penny's thoughts wandered to how much she despised them. She had made a mistake last week at Sunday dinner. When she saw the brussels sprouts on her plate she had said they looked like little green fungus balls. Mother and Father made her eat an extra one and declare that it was the best little green fungus ball she had ever eaten. They told her that brussels sprouts were good for her and they all needed to keep their resistance up. That thought brought her back to why she'd been thinking about brussels sprouts in the first place: sickness.

A deadly virus was sweeping the country. Influenza. Some teachers were sick. Some students were sick. Parents, brothers and sisters were sick. Worse than that, many people were dying. It seemed that everyone they knew either had someone with the Influenza or had a father, brother or uncle in the Great War in Europe. Some had both. Lots of soldiers were dying from the Influenza. Schools were being closed to try and stop the spread of the awful sickness.

Then, in a wave, Penny's brussels sprouts sensation went away and the sweet chocolate taste came back. No school! No school on her birthday! October 4, 1918—the day she'd turn twelve years old. She started thinking about the shiny new 1918 penny she would get for her collection. It had been hidden somewhere in the house, all year long, waiting for October 4.

Suddenly, Penny rolled forward onto her knees and started rapping on the window. Her best friend was walking by. Her name was Henny, or Henrietta when she was in trouble, which wasn't nearly as often as Penny. They were so frequently together that the boys referred to them as one, "Hennyandpenny." "Here comes Hennyandpenny," they'd say. Henny looked up with a big smile and gave an exaggerated wave. Penny motioned for her to come in. As she raced down the stairs from her bedroom, the front bell rang. She was almost at the front door when Mother walked into the foyer.

"How in the world did you get down here so fast after the bell rang?"

"A strange thing happened. I had a vision that Henny was standing at the front door about to ring the bell. Let's see how good I am." Penny flung the door wide open to show her friend standing there. "Aha!" Just as I saw it!"

"You really have the gift, honey. I think I'd call it the gift of having a bedroom with a window seat overlooking the front sidewalk." Mother laughed, said hello to Henny, and went back to her supper preparations.

"Come on in! What were you doing down there?"

"I was coming over here to see you. I'm so excited—I feel like it's my birthday tomorrow, not yours. No school! We can play on your birthday!"

"My mother said we could celebrate my birthday at lunch time and my father would come home. Now I don't have to wait until night time to get my presents! And, my mother said that you could come over. Do you think you can?"

"I know my parents will say yes to that. What do you think you're getting for your birthday?"

"There's one thing I know I'm getting—a penny!"

"A penny? How come?"

"You didn't move here 'til after my birthday last year. Come on up to my room and I'll show you. I get a penny every year on my birthday."

Penny grabbed Henny's arm and the two of them ran up the stairs. Penny opened up a dresser drawer and pulled out a small wooden box. She lifted the lid, showing her collection of pennies. "Can you guess why I get a penny on my birthday? I'll give you a hint, if you'd like."

"I like guessing games. Just give me a small hint."

"What's in a name? That's your hint!"

"Hmm . . . my mother quotes that from *Romeo and Juliet*. I think it goes on something like 'a rose by any other name is still a rose.' But you said you get a penny, not a rose. What does that have to do with anything?" asked Henny.

"It's not that complicated. I didn't even know they said that in *Romeo and Juliet*. How about this—what's in *my* name?"

"Your name? Oh! It's Penny! How silly of me."

"My parents named me Penelope just so that I could have the nickname Penny. I was named after my father's job. He works at the U.S. Mint where they make the money."

"I'm glad I wasn't named after my father's job. He's a plumber. What would my name have been?" Henny rolled her eyes.

"Well, I'm glad my parents didn't name me Nickelodeon, like the first movie theater, so that they could call me Nickel," giggled Penny.

"My first penny is from 1909, when the Lincoln penny came out. The new penny gave my father the idea of starting a collection for me. He gets a penny from the first batch minted in the year and saves it until my birthday. Tomorrow, I'll get a penny from the first batch of 1918."

Henny wrinkled up her nose. "I smell something good. It must be getting close to supper. I'd better go home."

Penny walked Henny to the front door and then followed the aroma to the kitchen. "What's for supper?" she asked Mother. She looked at the chart on the wall from the government that said RE-MEMBER THE DAYS. "Let's see . . . Thursday: one meal wheatless, one meal meatless. I haven't had any meat yet today. Do I smell meat?"

"You do indeed. It's roast chicken with carrots and potatoes, although we could have potatoes anytime. We were told, 'when in doubt, eat potatoes!' All these rules with eating make it tricky to plan a family's meals."

"How can it make any difference in the war for us to follow this silly schedule?"

"The government's trying to avoid food rationing. It's a lot easier to follow the meatless, wheatless schedule than to be given ration coupons for limited amounts of certain foods. The United States has been sending a lot of food over to Europe. It's the least we can do for the war effort."

At dinner, the conversation centered on The Great War overseas and then came closer to home with the influenza outbreak. Mother had been a nurse and was thankful they finally canceled school.

"I don't understand why they didn't cancel the parade for the Liberty Loan Drive last week. I'm all for buying bonds to support the war, but they should never have gone ahead with the parade. There were hundreds of thousands of people all close together, spreading germs. Now the Influenza is raging through Philadelphia like wildfire."

As Mother and Father continued their serious discussion, Penny tried to get lost in her sweet chocolate world. The only problem was that it reminded her that her birthday cake wouldn't be having chocolate frosting on it. Mother said that people were leaving chocolate frosting off cakes, as their part in helping the Belgian people not starve. She agreed to it, knowing she needed to do her part, but she was having trouble getting the connection between frosting on her birthday cake and starving Belgians. She was open to the idea of putting frosting on her cake and then inviting hungry Belgians over to eat some cake! Better yet, wasn't Brussels in Belgium? Why couldn't the Belgians just fill up on brussels sprouts?

Later, when Penny settled into bed for the evening, she found her head muddled with thoughts.

She said prayers for the soldiers fighting in Europe and for the sick people in this country. She hoped she got extra credit for praying for the hungry people in Belgium. Then she thought about how she didn't have to get up for school on her birthday and how Henny would be coming over for the day. That would be the frosting on her cake.

***

A little before noon the next day, Penny got into position on her window seat. She was on the lookout for Father and Henny. She spotted Father walking hurriedly down the street with a handkerchief in front of his face. He looked like he was about to sneeze, but he never took the handkerchief away. She ran downstairs and flung open the door. Father immediately put his handkerchief away and scooped her up.

"You were still sleeping when I left this morning. I haven't been able to say 'happy birthday' yet. How's my birthday girl?"

"No school on my birthday! That's how I'm doing! But Father, why did you have a handkerchief over your face?"

"I just thought I'd protect myself from any germs on the walk home. But it's your birthday, so no talk of that today. Is Henny here yet?"

"Not yet. I've been playing a game by the window to see which one of you got here first. You won! But, here she is now—a close second." Henny was heading toward them, swinging a small bag in each hand.

"There's my other girl! It's not a party without Henny and Penny!"

"Happy Birthday, Penny! This sure is better than going to school!"

As they walked into the dining room, Penny noticed that one of Henny's small bags had a pretty pink hair ribbon tied around it. Henny put it on the sideboard next to a couple of small presents Mother had put there earlier. The other bag was plain; she put it under her chair at the table.

"Does your birthday lunch stick to the "meatless and wheatless" rules?" asked Henny.

"Yes. Today is Friday, so it's one meatless meal and one wheatless meal. I love tomato sandwiches so I thought our lunch could be meatless. Our victory garden still has some ripe tomatoes on the vine so my mother made fresh tomato sandwiches."

"I love tomato sandwiches. I hope you don't mind tomato juice dripping down my chin."

"You'll be in good company," Father said. "I'm sure we'll all have juice dripping down our chins. Let's enjoy juicy tomatoes while we can. I'm sure we'll have a frost soon, and that will be the end of the season for the victory garden."

Penny had resigned herself to a very plain birthday cake, but her face lit up when Mother carried in a beautiful cake on one of the good china platters. The cake had been decorated with autumn flowers from the garden, making it one of the prettiest cakes Penny had ever seen.

"Would you like to give your present first, Henny?" asked Father.

"May I save mine for last?"

"Sure. In that case, I believe I have something in my pocket for Penny." Father reached into his pocket.

"Is that the same pocket your handkerchief is in?" Penny asked, worriedly.

"No, I made sure I didn't do that," laughed Father. He handed her a tiny drawstring bag. She pulled it open, anxious to see a shiny new penny for her collection. Instead, she saw a piece of candy.

"It's a penny candy. Aren't you collecting penny candies?" asked Father.

"I could never collect penny candies. I'd eat each one before I ever had two in my collection!"

"Why don't you look and see if there's anything else in the bag?"

Sure enough, there was a sparkling 1918 penny in the bottom of the bag. Penny jumped up and gave Father a kiss. "Pennies I *can* collect!"

While Penny showed her new penny to Henny, Mother went to the sideboard to retrieve two more gifts. Penny slipped her new penny into her pocket for safekeeping. She picked up a small packet and shook it. It made a jingling sound. She was sure these were the twenty-five cents she asked for to buy war stamps. They wouldn't be shiny ones, from the first press of the year, but they'd pay for war stamps just the same. She'd seen posters showing boys and girls buying war stamps, just like the adults were buying war bonds. She emptied the packet onto the table and admired the pile of pennies.

"I trust you, but I think I'll count them for the fun of it." She counted them two at a time, knowing there'd be one left over when she got to twenty-four. But, as Penny counted, she got to twenty-six, twenty-eight, thirty, and on. She looked up at Mother in amazement as she counted higher and higher. She continued counting by twos and ended up exactly at fifty. "Fifty cents!"

"Twenty-five cents for stamps and twenty-five cents for you! Now, go ahead and open the other present."

Penny eagerly unwrapped the next gift. She was amazed to find a beautiful leather-bound copy of the book, *Little Women*, by Louisa May Alcott.

"We won't be borrowing books from the library while the Influenza is taking over Philadelphia. With school canceled, you'll have plenty of time to read. It's a special gift for my own little woman."

After hugging and kissing Mother, Penny saw that Henny had set her gift on the table.

"It's just something simple that I made for you with something we had at home. I hope you'll have fun with it."

Penny untied the pink hair ribbon and used it to pull her copper locks into a ponytail. She tossed her head around, with exaggeration, for everyone to admire the effect. She then opened the bag and pulled out a long rope.

"It's a jump rope," declared Henny. "We had a long rope in our cellar, and my mother said I could cut it into a jump rope for you. My father helped me burn the edges so they wouldn't fray. There was enough rope left over for me to make one for myself, too. That's what I have in the bag under my chair. Now we can jump rope together!"

"Thank you so much, Henny! May we be excused to go outside and jump rope?"

"Of course! Go outside and have some fun. Why don't you jump rope in the back yard? You never know who might be walking by on the front side-walk and what germs they might have. I'm sorry to be such a worrier, but I'd feel better if you stayed out back." Mother's nursing instincts had taken over.

As the girls started jumping rope, Penny asked Henny if she had heard the new jump rope song during recess. "It has something to do with the Influenza. I don't remember exactly how it goes. Did you hear it?"

"I did, and since I knew I'd be giving you a jump rope, I asked some of the girls to teach it to me," said Henny. "This is how it goes:"

I had a bird and his name was Enza

I opened the window and

In-flu-enza.

The girls spent the afternoon playing in the backyard. They jumped rope to the new song and to others they already knew. They made up their own jumping song about Henny and Penny. They practiced cartwheels across the lawn. They raked leaves into piles and jumped into them.

They were worn out by the time Henny left for home and Penny went in for supper. After a wheatless dinner of vegetable beef soup, she washed up and went to her room.

Penny then did her favorite birthday evening ritual. She took out her collection of pennies. She lined the pennies up on her dresser, starting with the

1909 penny. She reached into her pocket to add the new 1918 penny in its place.

Penny's heart began to pound. Where was her penny? She pulled her pocket inside out. There was nothing in there but fragments of leaves which crumbled to the floor. She emptied her left pocket, though she clearly remembered putting the penny into her right pocket with her right hand. More leaf debris littered the floor. Penny started to panic.

Why did I put the penny in my pocket? she asked herself. Why didn't I put it back in the bag it came in? What am I going to do? She fought back tears as she thought of all the places in the backyard that she and Henny had been. She didn't have the heart to tell Mother and Father. She tried to calm down as she told herself that maybe she would find the penny. Henny would probably help her look for it. At least they didn't have school the next day and would be able to spend time in the backyard.

When Penny went to bed that night, she tried to focus on the wonderful birthday she had had and not the penny that she had lost. It took her awhile, but eventually she drifted off to sleep.

***

At breakfast the next morning, Penny was given permission to go straight to Henny's house, although Mother and Father had no idea what her rush was all about. She was given the now familiar lecture about not stopping anywhere else, not visiting anyone else's house, not stopping to talk to anyone and not picking anything up off the street.

Penny stood at attention and saluted Mother in response to all of her health regulations. "At ease," commanded Mother.

It was only a few, familiar blocks and turns to Henny's house, but the route had a different feel this morning. Anyone out on the streets seemed to be walking with a definite purpose; no one was just hanging around. Penny knew people had lots of worries these days, but she was consumed with her own troubles. She was sick to her stomach over her missing penny.

Penny took Henny's front steps two at a time and impatiently rapped the brass doorknocker, like an SOS message being sent in Morse code. She paced the landing as she waited for the door to open.

"Who's there?" Henny's mother said from the other side of the door.

Penny thought it was odd that the door stayed closed. "It's me, Penny. Can Henny come over to play?"

The door opened a crack and Penny could just make out a portion of the usually friendly face of her friend's mother. There was no smile today. She looked strange, not at all like herself.

"Oh, Penny! Henrietta is sick. She's in bed with a fever. I'm so worried it's the Influenza. And you were with her all day yesterday."

Penny gasped and then felt like the air was sucked right back out of her. Once she caught her breath, her words came out in a tumble. "But she was fine yesterday. Is she okay? Will she be okay? What can I do? Can I get something? My mother was a nurse—should I get her?"

"I'd like to talk to your mother, but I won't let her come in. Your family's been exposed enough."

"Please tell Henny that I hope she feels better. I'll go get my mother. She can talk to you at the door."

Penny's thoughts raced along with her feet on the way home. Was it the Influenza? How sick would Henny get? So many people never got better. Would she get it? Would her parents get it?

She felt her throat start to burn, her mouth quiver and knew that next her eyes would be filling with tears. By the time she ran into her house and found Mother, she had worked herself into such a state that she couldn't speak an intelligible word.

Mother put a hand on each of her heaving shoulders, as if steadying a rocking canoe. "What's wrong, Penny? What happened? Are you okay? Calm down, take a deep breath and tell me what's going on!"

Penny took a deep breath and tried again. "It's Henny! She's sick with a fever. Her mother doesn't know whether it's the Influenza or not. She'll only open the door a little bit, but she'd like to talk to you. Can we go back over?"

"Oh, no. Poor Henny. You'll stay right here. I'll go over. I'll carry over some of the broth from the soup left over from dinner last night. While I'm gone you can draw a picture and write a note to her. We'll drop it off another time."

Penny knew better than to argue with Mother. She helped her strain the broth from the soup into a small pot. After Mother left, Penny sat down to write to Henny. She was so caught up in the seriousness of it that she accidentally wrote "Dear Henrietta" the first time. She started over with "Dear Henny." She tried to sound cheerful. She didn't even tell her about the lost penny. She'd actually forgotten about the penny until just then. It didn't seem to matter anymore.

Late in the afternoon, Penny and Mother walked back to Henny's house. Mother explained that overnight would tell a lot more about how Henny was doing. She said that it might be the Influenza because it came on so quickly, which was how it struck. If Henny didn't take a turn for the worse overnight or in the next few days, then maybe she had a milder case or some other virus. Mother explained that people with Influenza often had such high fevers that they became delirious, talking nonsense in their sleep, while they sweated through their bedclothes.

"If she's so sick, shouldn't she go to the hospital?"

"The hospitals were understaffed even before this influenza epidemic hit. Most of the medical personnel have gone off to Europe to help in The Great War. The hospitals are filled with sick and dying patients and very few people to care for them. I've felt guilty for not going back as a nurse to help out, but I would feel guiltier bringing the Influenza home to you."

They knocked on the door and slipped Penny's note and picture to Henny's mother through the crack. She told them that Henny was about the same, but she'd been able to keep down some of the broth. They'd been following Mother's instructions about wet cloths and liquids. Penny and Mother promised to check back with them in the morning.

Penny went to bed early, partly because she didn't feel like doing anything else and partly to make the morning come sooner.

When Penny went downstairs in the morning, Mother was already in the kitchen with a pot of chicken broth on the stove. She informed her that she wasn't going to have Penny walking back and forth to Henny's house, wearing herself out. She would deliver the chicken soup herself and let

Penny know how her friend was doing. Left with little choice, Penny picked up her new book and decided to spend the day in her window seat.

Before she opened her book, she stared out her window to the street below. It was just a few days ago that Henny was down there waving to her. The clippety-clop of a horse-drawn cart caught her attention. The sight of its load filled Penny with dread. The cart was piled high with caskets. Each one, another person lost to the Influenza. She rubbed her eyes, as if erasing the image, and opened her book to escape into another world.

Penny was so engrossed in her reading that she hadn't seen Mother walk down the street or heard her enter the house. She looked up, startled, as her bedroom door opened. She snapped into the present.

"How is she?"

"Henrietta still has a high fever and is a sick girl, but her body really seems to be fighting whatever she's got. She's been sleeping a lot, but her mother said she sleeps peacefully and is clear-headed when she's awake. I think that's good news. She sent a message back to you, thanking you for your note and picture. She said she's looking forward to the next one."

"Do you think I could use the telephone to call and talk with her sometime?"

"Well, aside from the fact that she shouldn't get out of bed to get to the telephone, the Telephone Company has lost so many of its employees to the Influenza that calls are being restricted to emergencies only. It seems that everything is being affected by this horrible epidemic. Why don't you get back to your book? I'm going to go downstairs and put my feet up for awhile."

The next morning, when Penny was still in bed, there was an early knock on the door. She threw back her covers and ran across the floor to her window seat. She pressed her face against the cool window to see who was at the door. Henny's father! What could that be about? She ran downstairs, not even worrying that she was still in her nightgown. Mother hadn't worried either. Penny could see the back of her nightgown as she talked to Henny's father through the slightly opened door. She ran up behind Mother, and tugged on her nightgown.

"What is it? Why is Henny's father here? Is she okay?"

Mother turned to face Penny. "I'll excuse your interruption because I know how worried you are. It's good news! Hear it for yourself!" She stepped aside and opened the door a bit more.

"Hello, Penny. I know it's very early to stop by, but I had to share the wonderful news with you. Henny's fever broke during the night! She seems to be over the worst of it. She'll still need time to rest and recover so she won't be jumping rope with you any time soon. But, it looks like she's going to be alright."

Penny felt that throat-burning, mouth-quivering feeling again and knew the tears were on their way. She had been frozen with fear over what news had brought Henny's father to their house so early. She hung on to Mother and let her tears of relief soak into her nightgown. Mother thanked Henny's father for coming over, and closed the door.

***

The next few weeks were spent quietly. Thousands of people were dying in Philadelphia alone.

There were no more trips to Henny's house. There was so much sickness and death around the city that the family stayed at home. Penny was able to make a few telephone calls to find out that Henny was gaining her strength.

One afternoon, Penny was curled up in a chair in the living room, re-reading her precious copy of *Little Women.* She found herself identifying with the character, Jo. She thought about losing her penny, and told herself that Jo might have done something like that. She heard Mother and Father talking in the background.

Father spoke of the city running out of caskets for burying the dead. He said that so many grave-diggers were sick that people had to dig graves for their own family members. He said more young soldiers were dying from the Influenza than from the fighting itself.

"I can't believe I'm going to say this, but I'm actually starting to miss school. When do you think they might be able to reopen?"

"I don't know," Father replied. "The authorities are keeping track of the numbers of sick and dying. They have said when they start to see a drop in the

71

numbers then they can assume the epidemic is winding down. The only way to contain it is to try to keep people from gathering together and spreading germs. Maybe you'll appreciate school more when it reopens."

"I know I will. I've learned a lot of lessons lately."

***

As quickly as the Influenza had come upon Philadelphia, it seemed to miraculously disappear. By the end of October, schools and churches opened again. Life went back to its normal routine for Penny. Henny was well enough to go back to school when it reopened.

Early on a Monday morning, just a few weeks after returning to school, Penny was in a deep sleep. She was having a strange dream about firemen putting out fires while on their way to church. She felt herself waking up out of the dream, as if she were swimming up from deep water. When she finally rose to the surface, she realized the church

72

bells were still ringing. She looked towards the window. It was still dark out, with just a hint of dawn. She remembered it was Monday. Why were church bells ringing? She moaned and pulled her quilt over her head. Then Penny heard sirens wailing outside her window. Were firemen really on their way to church? Penny climbed out of bed and groped her way to Mother and Father's bedroom. They were already at the door.

"What's going on? What's all the noise about?"

"We don't know. Let's go downstairs and see what we can find out."

They all walked down the stairs and to the front door. When they looked out the door, they couldn't believe what was going on. Outside, in the early morning hours, as church bells rang and sirens blared, neighbors were dancing in the streets! This was even stranger than her dream. Penny pinched herself. Yes, she was definitely awake.

Father ran outside and talked to one of the neighboring men. Then he hugged him. He came running back, grabbing both Mother and Penny and enveloping them in an enormous hug.

"It's over! The war is over!"

Before Penny knew it, she was out on the street hugging and dancing with Mother, Father and the neighbors. She realized that just like the morning when she found out that Henny was better, she was being seen in her nightgown. She didn't care. She wasn't the only one. The Great War was over! What a scene there was in the street. People were dressed in all sorts of things and making noise with anything they could get their hands on. Penny ran back in the house to get pots and spoons. The three of them joined an impromptu parade and began cheering and banging as they marched down the street.

Father yelled over the noise that he'd heard that a document was signed in France declaring the war to be over. Fighting was to end at 11:00 a.m., France time.

"Do you realize what that means, Penny? Today is actually November 11th. The fighting will end at the eleventh hour of the eleventh day of the eleventh month!"

Penny thought that if this had been just a few weeks earlier, everyone might have quietly celebrated in their homes. She'd heard that in some cities the Influenza was still on the rise. She wondered how those cities were celebrating. But this was no quiet celebration. More and more people were joining in. Everyone was overcome with emotion; people were laughing, crying or doing both. Church bells throughout Philadelphia continued to ring.

That night, before going to bed, Penny pulled out her penny collection. There were many times since her birthday that she had felt sick about having lost her 1918 penny. Today, though, Penny realized that it wasn't such a big deal. The end of the Influenza outbreak and the end of The Great War—those are big deals, she thought. That lost penny can be a reminder of all the lives lost in 1918. It can also remind me of the special feeling of today, Armistice Day—November 11, 1918.

Chapter 5

IN FOR A PENNY, IN FOR A POUND

Michael drummed his fingers on top of his bent knees as he sat on the sidewalk in front of school. His feet beat along to the rhythm that was pulsating through him from his earphones. His eyes were closed and his head leaned back against the hard brick wall. Every now and then he opened his eyes and scanned the carpool line. It was easy to get lost in the jazz that tap-danced its way into his head and through his whole body. Easy to get lost and hard to keep still.

Man, if he could only play his saxophone like that. He'd get a solo in the band concert for sure. He'd be up on the stage with his eyes shut and his entire body would be playing the sax. When the song ended, he'd open his eyes and the audience would be on their feet, clapping and cheering wildly. A boy could dream.

"Hey kid! Need a ride?"

His reverie ended when he opened his eyes and saw Dad smiling through the rolled down passenger window of his car. Michael turned off the music, swung his backpack over his shoulder and picked up his saxophone case. He put his gear in the back seat and then climbed in the front with Dad.

"You were in another world. I actually waited a couple minutes to see if you'd open your eyes before I called out. I could almost feel your music through the foot-stomping and finger-tapping. What were you listening to?"

"The band instructor lent me a CD by Duke Ellington. Man, could he play! We're gonna do a whole medley of jazz for the fall concert. I'm trying to get my nerve up to try out for a solo. I wanna play 'Take the "A" Train.' Do you know it?"

"Know it? That's a classic. My dad used to play it on the record player all the time. He and my mom would dance around the living room. I can still see them now. You need to go for that solo. You know what it takes: practice, practice, practice!"

"Hmmm, seems like I've heard that somewhere before. You'll get sick of the song with as much as I have to practice."

"I don't think I could ever get tired of those old jazz greats. What else are you up to? What did you stay after school for today—band?"

"No, today was the school newspaper. It was a kind of jam session, just not the musical kind. Everybody was tossing out ideas for articles. They liked my idea. I'm gonna write about the social studies project my class has to do. We all have to look for old pennies and then research the year of the oldest penny we find. I'm gonna open up my old bank to see what I've got."

"Pennies! Have *I* got pennies! Remember that gumball machine you and your sister got me for my birthday years ago?"

"Sure, I remember it. You took it to your office for fun. Whenever Leah and I went to visit you, you gave us pennies for gum."

"Well, you wouldn't believe how often that gumball machine gets used. I've filled it with more gumballs but I've never emptied the pennies out. It must be filled with pennies. I'll empty it tomorrow and bring the pennies home for you."

As they pulled into their driveway, Dad said, "Hey, you better get your homework done early. We've got a ball game to watch tonight!"

"I know! I wore my Yankees shirt for good luck today."

***

The next evening, a constant refrain of "Take the 'A' Train" resonated throughout the house. Michael struggled through one bar, playing it over and over again.

"At least shut your door! I'm going insane!" He heard Leah slam his door and stomp down the hall. She didn't get jazz at all. Little sisters didn't seem to get much of anything. He took a deep breath and resumed his playing.

He felt like things were beginning to click when he heard banging on his door. He opened it to see Leah standing there.

"You can't hear anything when you're playing that thing. Mom and Dad made me come up to get you for dinner. Hey, didn't you wear that same shirt yesterday? That's pretty gross."

"It's my lucky Yankees shirt. It worked yesterday so I had to wear it again today. It doesn't smell. Get over it." She really didn't get anything.

"Mom, Michael wore the same shirt two days in a row. Tell him that's gross," Leah whined, once they were downstairs.

Dad high-fived Michael. "Way to go! Let's see if it's as charmed today as it was yesterday." Dad definitely got it.

Mom shook her head. "Michael, give me the shirt after the game tonight and I'll wash it. If it's too late then I'll throw it in the dryer tomorrow morning before school. I guess if they win tonight you'll need it again tomorrow." Mom sort of got it.

"Michael, I'll need your help getting something out of my armored car after dinner."

"What armored car? Did you pull off a bank heist today?" He asked with a laugh.

"Something like that. Let's help clear the table and then I'll show you."

"The 'goods' are in the backseat," Dad said, in the tone of a tough criminal in an old movie.

A few minutes later, Michael peered through the car window into the backseat. There was a lumpy plastic bag on the smooth leather seat. He opened the door and reached in to pick it up. It was a lot heavier than he expected.

"Oh, the goods!" he said, in his best crime boss accent. "You kept your end of the bargain, so I won't have to get rough with you. I'll give you your cut when I make sure it's the real stuff."

Back in the house, Michael set the bag on the kitchen table. He reached in and his hands filled up with coins.

"Hey, there are even some nickels, dimes and quarters in here. Some people must have been pretty desperate for a piece of gum!" Michael laughed.

"I always knew I worked with some desperate people! But I didn't realize I had a profitable side business in gumballs."

The whole family was hovering around Michael and the bag of coins. He decided he'd let everyone help look through the pennies. Otherwise he'd be there all night and he still wanted to practice his sax before watching the baseball game. Leah wanted to look for all the nickels, dimes and quarters and count them.

"Once Michael finds his old penny, what can we do with the rest of the money?" Leah was eyeing her growing stash.

Dad tapped his fingers on the table. "Let's see. The gumball machine was a gift to me and I bought the refill gumballs. If I have any say in the matter, which I'm guessing I don't, then I think all the money should be mine to keep!"

"Come on, Dad, that's no fun. Can't we buy or do something with all this money?" Leah begged.

"I might be convinced to take everyone out for ice cream or order pizza one night. Let's wait and see what it adds up to be."

"Let's divide them up into different decades— the '80s, '70s, or whatever." Michael started sorting the pennies in his hand. "It'll be cool to see how the piles end up."

Mom got some pieces of paper and wrote the decades on top of each. As everyone sorted through their pennies they watched which pieces of paper became covered.

"Well, I'm not surprised that most of the pennies are from more recent years, but there are more from the fifties than I expected," Mom observed. "You could do some research on rock and roll!"

Michael jumped out of his chair, nearly knocking it over. "Forget the '50s! Look what I have! I can't believe it! I've got a penny from 1927!"

"1927!" exclaimed Dad. "That's the year my dad was born. That's amazing!"

"I wonder what happened that year," Michael pondered. "I forgot to tell you what our teacher said about holding the penny in our hand. Once we research the year, we're supposed to imagine a kid like us who might have had it in his hand and what was going on around him." Michael slowly closed his hand around his 1927 penny.

Chapter 6

LUCKY PENNY

Joseph sat on the front steps of his apartment building, kicking at a loose stone, feeling sorry for himself. "I's nearly a teenager, now, but it ain't doin' me no good," he grumbled to himself. His mind was on the latest shaking dance move that everyone was talking about: the heebie-jeebies. "The only shakin' I got going on is my foot on this here step." He felt like the lively action of Harlem was a parade passing him right by.

Harlem seemed like the center of everything to Joseph, but he still felt like he was on the outside of it all. He wanted to be able to go in the clubs, listen to the music and really get the heebie-jeebies. But he wasn't old enough to get in any of the clubs, and he wasn't even the right color to get into The Cotton Club. It ain't fair, he thought, that the only way colored folk can get in there is if they be workin' there—playin' their music, waitin' on white folk or cleanin' up after 'em.

"Sittin' there feelin' sorry for yo'self?" Mama asked him. Even that annoyed Joseph; she could read his mind. "Ain't gonna do much good. I tried it myself after your daddy done died in The Great War. I was sad—I'd lost my husband and my baby's daddy—and I was mad—he died fightin' for a country that may have freed my grandparents from slavery, but still slammed doors in our faces. But that anger and sadness was only draggin' us down. It took my own mama to remind me that she and my daddy and their folks before that, all put one foot in front of the other jus' to make it through the day—keepin' faith that things'd get better. Jus' like I'm tellin' you now that you need to get up, put one foot in front of the other and do somethin' 'bout makin' things better. Harlem is filled with hope right now. It's like a fever that's spreadin', honey. Right here in Harlem, there are colored writers, poets, singers, dancers, jazz musicians and business folk. White folk are spendin' good money to come to Harlem to listen to our music. Florence Mills has even taken her singin' and dancin' to Paris. If ever there was a time and place for us to have hope, child, it's now—September 1927, right here in Harlem!"

"Mama, I's sorry. What can I do? I feel like all these happenin's is goin' on 'round me and I don't have no part in it. I wanna *do* somethin'. What can I do?"

"Maybe it's time you be gettin' yo'self a job after school. But I tell you what. School comes first. That's the ticket you need if you wanna get on the train that's comin' through now. Else, it's gonna pass you right by. But I don't see no harm in you earnin' a few pennies of your own. It won't hurt for you to do your part in helpin' out me and your Aunt Sarah and Uncle Paul, either. When Aunt Sarah has her baby, she'll be staying home to take care of it. Things'll be tight when she stops workin'. What you say 'bout lookin' for a little job?"

Joseph liked the idea. He wondered what kind of job he could get. Maybe he could sweep or clean somewhere. Maybe he could sweep or clean at The Cotton Club!

"Mama! You think I could get a job doin' some cleanin' up at The Cotton Club?"

Mama shook her head back and forth. "I do not. That's no job for a boy, cleanin' up who knows what after a wild night at that joint! What about seein' if they need any help at the Negro newspaper. You know, *The Amsterdam News*? Why don't you go by after school tomorrow? It's gettin' late out here now and you know how hard it is to get your sorry self out of bed for school," Mama said, poking him playfully. "Let's be goin' on in now. Feelin' any better?"

"I guess. We'll see what happens tomorrow."

As Joseph got ready for bed, he listened to the quiet voices of Mama talking with Aunt Sarah and Uncle Paul. It wouldn't be long before she came to bed too. Her bed was on the other side of an old sheet hanging in the middle of the bedroom. He had trouble settling down, thinking about looking for a job after school the next day. After awhile, he heard Mama tiptoe into the other side of the room, thinking that he was asleep. When he heard the steady breathing of her deep sleep, he finally relaxed into slumber as well.

***

The next day at school, Joseph had more trouble paying attention than usual. He was trying to figure out what to say when he went by the newspaper office after school. How could he convince them to hire him? What if they didn't have any jobs? He needed to be able to give them some ideas of things he could do. He knew that there might be a news-boy job for him to sell newspapers. But he really wanted to be inside the office, where he could see and listen to the people who wrote and worked for the paper. Then, he could hear the latest news before it even made it into the paper that was sold on the streets.

At last, the school day ended and it was time to go to *The Amsterdam News* office. He turned left outside of the school, instead of his usual right to go home. Suddenly, his feet felt like lead.

"Hey, Joseph. Where you goin' this afternoon? How come you're not turnin' towards home," asked a boy who lived in the same apartment building.

Joseph didn't answer right away. He didn't want anyone to know he was looking for a job. He didn't want them to try to get a job at the same place, and he didn't want to be embarrassed in case he didn't get a job.

"I got an errand to run for my mama. I'll be home in a little while. See you later." Joseph got his feet in motion.

He'd been excited all day, but now he found himself taking very slow, shuffling steps. As long as he wasn't talking to anyone there yet, he could still hang on to the hope that he might get a job. He finally arrived at the front door of the office and took a deep breath. He walked up to the woman sitting behind a desk in the front area.

"'Scuse me ma'am. I was wonderin' if you had any positions for a hard workin' boy, uh, I mean, young man? Um, what I mean is I'd be wantin' to do anything around the office that might need doin', like cleanin' up or errands . . . or anything!"

Later, Joseph would think about how he had been standing exactly where he should be, at exactly the right time. Those slow, shuffling steps on the way to *The Amsterdam News* must have been timed just right. Because just as the woman behind the desk opened her mouth and started to say, "I'm sorry, but I don't know of any—" she was inter-rupted by a woman who walked up behind Joseph.

"So you're looking for a position, young man?" He turned in the direction of the voice and saw the woman standing there.

"Yes, ma'am."

"I'm Mrs. Warren. What's your name?"

"I'm Joseph."

"I was just thinking that it sure would be handy to have someone do odd jobs that come up. Things like running papers between departments, sharpen-ing pencils, emptying out pencil sharpeners, things like that. Tell me, why are you the one for the job?"

Joseph was ready for this question. This is what he had thought about all day in school. This is what got him in trouble when Miss Morris called on him and he hadn't had any idea what she had asked.

"Ma'am, I wanna be in the action. I wanna see and hear 'bout everything that's happenin' in Harlem. Seems to me that somethin's goin' on all the time here. And I work hard and do as I's told, I mean, I'm told."

"I think we can keep you busy here. School comes first, though, so it will have to be after school. What about two hours after school each day?" she asked him.

"Ma'am, that sound jus' right. Thank you, ma'am. When can I start?"

"Are you accepting the job without knowing how much it pays?" The woman laughed.

Joseph felt his face burn. He realized he'd have taken the job for free, but decided not to let her know that. He had no idea how much money he'd get paid.

"I's, I mean, I'm sorry, ma'am. This be my first job, so I forgot to ask that."

"Well, I wish we could give you more, but after each day you've worked your two hours, stop by the front desk and you'll get 25 cents. As long as you're here now, why don't we give you a tour of our offices? You can do a little work after that, and we'll give you your first 25 cents."

Joseph was a sponge, soaking up everything he saw and heard. He felt like he was in the heartbeat of Harlem. He couldn't believe it was just last night that he sat on the front steps feeling sorry for himself. There was nothing to feel sorry about now! He felt like he must be the luckiest boy in Harlem, maybe even the whole world. After his tour, Mrs. Warren suggested he walk around the office and see if there were any odd jobs he could do. She told him when it was time for him to go that he should stop by the front desk. She'd arrange for his 25 cents to be there for him. He shook her hand like a real business man, and then walked around to see if anyone needed help.

"Well, hey there, boy! They sure are hiring reporters young these days. It looks like I'm gonna be havin' some competition for the hot stories," laughed a man at a desk. The man's desk was covered by piles of papers, pencils and erasers.

"I's, I mean, I'm not a reporter . . . yet!" Joseph said, with a smile. "I been hired to help out with odd jobs and errands." Then, Joseph remembered the manners which Mama reminded him to use today. "My name is Joseph. Is there anything I can help you with?"

"Hi, Joseph. Nice to meet you. My name's Benjamin, but you can call me Ben. It's gonna be great havin' some help 'round here. Make sure I don't take advantage of you!" Ben grinned.

Joseph liked Ben right away. He offered to sharpen the reporter's pencils. After helping out, he continued around the newsroom, meeting and helping other reporters.

At one desk, someone had a radio turned on with jazz music playing. Joseph tapped his foot to the music as he asked the reporter if he could sharpen his pencils or refill his coffee for him.

"I think I'm set, thanks. I see your foot tappin' to this here music. You like jazz?"

"I sure do. I keep wishin' I could get into a club. I know we're not allowed in The Cotton Club, but if I was older I could go some place like Small's Paradise. I like what's playin' now. Who's playin' it?"

"This is about the best there is. It's Duke Ellington. Duke likes to say, 'It don't mean a thing, if it ain't got that swing!' You got good taste in music, kid."

Joseph moved on, doing odd jobs for different reporters. He looked up at the clock and saw that his two hours were up. He couldn't wait to go home and tell Mama about his day. He realized he'd probably get home just around the same time as Mama did from her cleaning job.

He was nervous about getting his 25 cents. Did the lady know to give it to him or did he have to ask for it? How would he ask? He started his slow shuffle again as he tried to figure out how to ask for it. Suddenly, he heard his name.

"Joseph! How'd it go? Did they wear you out?" The lady at the front desk had a big smile for him.

"No, ma'am. Everybody was real nice to me."

She handed him his 25 cents without his having to say a word. He couldn't believe he had his very own money. Well, it wasn't really his money to keep. But he did earn it himself.

He couldn't wait to tell Mama, but first, he had to make a quick stop at the corner store. Joseph had decided to surprise her by bringing home something he bought with his first pay. He hesitated at the store's front window. It was filled with an array of items for sale. A shiny harmonica caught his eye. It had a price tag on it for 50 cents. Joseph couldn't believe that by the end of tomorrow he'd have enough money to buy it. But if he did that, he wouldn't be able to give Mama any money. He really wanted that harmonica, though. He decided he'd have to set aside a few pennies each day to save up for it.

Joseph looked around the store. He figured out if he bought a loaf of bread and a quart of milk he'd get one penny back in change. Maybe he could save a couple of pennies starting tomorrow. One penny was fine today, if he could walk into the apartment carrying a loaf of bread and a quart of milk. He bought his groceries from Mr. Morgan, the owner of the store. Joseph told him he was a working man now and he was surprising Mama with the groceries. He told him he was saving the penny change. Mr. Morgan told him that, in that case, he would give him a shiny new 1927 penny he'd just gotten from the bank.

Since Joseph had stopped at the store first, Mama had arrived home just before him. He ran up the steps with his bag from the store. No slow, shuffling steps this time.

"Mama, Mama! I got somethin' for you!"

"And hello to you, too. Where you been? It's not like you to not be here when I get home. It shouldn't be takin' this long if you stopped at the newspaper right after school. And what's in the bag?"

"Mama, you won't believe it! I got a job today, workin' at *The Amsterdam News*. I started today. A lady named Miz Warren hired me."

"The owner? You mean you met Miz Warren? The lady who bought the newspaper? Her husband had been the owner and she bought it when he died. Boy, how'd you do that?" Mama looked at him with awe.

"She jus' walked up while I was askin' 'bout a job. Then she ask me to start today, jus' doin' odd jobs and such. But I's gettin' paid each day after I work two hours. Here," he said as he handed Mama the bag. "This is for you, from my first pay."

Mama opened the bag and couldn't believe there were a quart of milk and a loaf of bread inside. She looked like she couldn't decide whether to laugh or cry.

"Son, you a real man now. I's so proud of you. But I want you to keep a little somethin' for yo'self too."

"I did. I kept a penny from today's work, and I'll be drinkin' some of that milk and eatin' some of that bread. I thought I'd try and save a couple pennies a day towards a harmonica. I saw one for 50 cents. You can tell me each mornin' if there is somethin' you need me to get on the way home from work."

"Honey, how 'bout you take your pay from the next two days and buy yo'self that harmonica. We'll work out somethin' with your pay helpin' us all out after that."

Joseph and Mama gave each other a big hug, then she pulled away from him and looked very serious.

"Don't be forgettin' that school comes first, young man. If I see that this job gets in the way of your schoolwork, you'll have to give it up—you understand?"

"I know, Mama. That's just what Miz Warren said, too."

"Your daddy'd be so proud of you."

***

Two days later, Joseph looked up at the clock in the newsroom of *The Amsterdam News*. It was nearly time for him to collect his 25 cents. He'd be heading straight to the corner store to buy that harmonica. He couldn't believe he'd have enough money to buy it himself. When his two hours were up, he stopped by the front desk where he was handed his pay.

"I've been hearing good things about you, Joseph. Everyone is real happy with the job you're doing. I heard the reporters joke that they might forget how to sharpen a pencil."

"Thank you, ma'am. I'm tryin' to do a real good job. I'll see you tomorrow." He walked politely out the door, but as soon as he was out of view he broke into a run. He stopped in front of the corner store to make sure the harmonica was still there.

You're waitin' for me, aren't you? Joseph asked the harmonica silently. We gonna have a good time together, jus' wait and see!

"Hi, Mr. Morgan." He put his 50 cents from two days' work on the counter by the cash register. "I'd like to buy that harmonica in the front window, please."

"Hi, Joseph. I'll go get it for you. No bread and milk for you today?"

"Not today! Mama said I could buy myself the harmonica before I go back to helpin' out with groceries."

Mr. Morgan went to the front window and took out the harmonica. He put it inside its box and handed it to Joseph. Joseph said goodbye and charged out of the store.

When he got home, he greeted Mama, Aunt Sarah and Uncle Paul, and then ran into the bedroom. He took the harmonica out of the box and began to blow into it. Joseph was disappointed that it didn't sound like the music coming out of the radio at work. He tried to hear the jazz music in his head as he blew into the harmonica. He started to think that it might sound like real music with a little practice.

Mama poked her head into the bedroom. "Those first few noises you were makin' had me thinkin' I'd done the wrong thing lettin' you buy that harmonica," she laughed. "But you know, it's already startin' to sound like a familiar song."

"Thanks, Mama. I was tryin' to play 'That's When I'll Come Back to You,' by Louis Armstrong."

"It sure was startin' to sound like somethin'. It'll be nice hearin' some music around here. It's time for some supper, Joseph. After that, you'll need to be doin' your homework."

"I don't have any homework tonight. I can just practice my harmonica after dinner," Joseph said happily.

***

Joseph got into a routine of stopping at the corner store after work, to pick up anything Mama might need. She had told him to save any change that he got. Whenever there was a penny or two left, Joseph put the coins in a jar in the bedroom. He was hoping he'd be able to buy some small Christmas presents for his family. He'd look in the store windows on his way home from work. He already picked out a bib as a present for when the baby was born. Joseph was hoping it would be a boy, because he saw a bib that had a baseball and bat pictured on it.

At work, one afternoon, Joseph walked by a desk where a group of reporters were standing and talking. It sounded like they were talking about baseball.

"Hey, Joseph! Stay here a minute. Let's hear your thinkin' on this," Ben said. "We're talking about the Negro Baseball League and the New York Yankees. The Chicago American Giants are about to play the Bacharach Giants in the Negro Baseball League's World Series, over in Jersey City. We're tryin' to figure out how either one of those teams would do up against the New York Yankees. You think either of 'em could beat the Yankees?"

All eyes of the reporters were on Joseph. "I really don't know. I hear lots about Willie Foster, the pitcher for the American Giants. I never been to a baseball game, though."

"You never been to a ball game? Let's see what we can do about that," said Ben. "I'll be headin' to the Negro World Series over in Jersey. Let me see if I can round up an extra ticket for you to go. If I can, do you think your parents would let you go with me?"

Joseph was stunned. "There's jus' Mama. I think she'd let me go. She might want to meet you first, though. You really think you can get a ticket for me?"

"I think so, but better yet, I've got another idea. If I can get two tickets, how about your mama goin' with us? Do you think she'd have any interest in goin' to a baseball game?"

The other reporters all laughed. One of them said, "You'll do anything for a date, Ben!" Another said, "You'd better watch out for Ben, Joseph!"

Joseph looked at Ben, wondering if he was looking for a date. Mama hadn't been out with anyone since Daddy had died. He was just a little boy back then. He'd never even thought about her going out on a date. He started to look at Ben in a different way. He liked him a lot and wouldn't mind him going out with Mama.

"Don't worry, Joseph. I'm not trying to take your mama out on a date. I just thought she might be more comfortable with you going to the game if she came along too. But it wouldn't hurt to know if she's a nice lady!"

"Mama is real nice and she's real pretty too. I think she'd like to get out to a baseball game. I don't think she's ever been to one, either."

"Well, you ask her how she feels about it, and I'll check around for two tickets. I might have to have one of these reporters give me one of theirs as payment for embarrassin' me just now."

Mama hadn't asked for anything from the store, so Joseph raced straight home after work. He wondered if he'd be able to use his money to buy a souvenir from the baseball game—that is, if he got to the baseball game.

"Mama! Mama! Guess what?" Joseph called out, as he opened the door to the apartment.

"You got more news for us? Every day we get some kind of a report about somethin' that's goin' on. "What's it today?"

"This is about us, not Harlem, New York or the United States. This is about us, Mama!"

"About us? What kinda news is about us?"

"You know how I told you about that nice reporter named Ben? Well, he said he'd try to get us tickets to the Negro Baseball League's World Series. Us, Mama—you and me!"

"Oh my! I's never been to a baseball game. I don't know how to act or anythin' about it. Maybe you should jus' go with him, without me taggin' along."

"Oh, Mama. I think it'd be fun for you to go too. Ben is real nice. He won't make you feel funny about anythin'. He'll probably teach you all about baseball. Can we go, please?"

"If this Ben can get tickets, then we can go. I guess I'd be a fool turnin' down a chance to go out somewhere special like that."

***

That night Joseph heard some great jazz playing while sitting in his room. He looked out the window and saw a party in an apartment across the street. The windows were wide open, since it was a warm, autumn evening. He could see a man across the street playing the saxophone. People were dressed up and going into the building. He ran to Mama in the kitchen.

"Mama, what's goin' on across the street? There's some kind of a party with live jazz. What is it?"

"That's what they be callin' a rent party. Somebody hires a jazz player to play in their apartment, then charges money for people to come listen and dance. They call it a rent party cuz they use the money to pay the rent!"

"I can just stick my head out the window and listen without payin' a thing."

As he listened to the jazz music, he played his harmonica along with it. He imagined himself standing right next to the saxophone player, with everyone having the heebie-jeebies because of music he was playing. He pictured folks piling out of the "A" train to see him at The Cotton Club or Small's Paradise. They would be dressed in their finest clothes and jewelry, with women hanging on the arms of the men. Joseph would love to be on the inside of Small's Paradise. It was famous for its roller skating waiters who would dance the latest rage, the Charleston, while they carried drinks on trays. Joseph heard that in Chicago there was a club that was also called The Cotton Club, and it was owned by a gangster named Al Capone. He and a lot of other criminals were making a lot of money from selling illegal alcohol. Joseph thought about all these things as he played his harmonica along with the music from the rent party.

The next day at work, Joseph was nervous about seeing Ben. He was afraid that he would tell him that he couldn't get tickets. He kept checking in with all the reporters except Ben, putting off any bad news he might have.

"Joseph! I haven't seen you all afternoon," said Ben as he walked up behind him. "What did your mama say about the baseball game? Those other reporters didn't scare you off from asking her, did they?"

"No, I couldn't wait to ask her! She said yes. But, do you think you'll be able to get tickets?"

"Already done! A couple folks owed me some favors. The three of us'll be taking a bus over to the game. How does that sound?"

"Great! Thanks so much, Ben. I'd better get to work now, before I lose my job, though."

***

Joseph was about to burst with excitement the day of the ball game. Even just taking the bus ride with Mama and Ben to Atlantic City was an adventure. Mama was a little more shy than usual but Ben was as nice and funny as ever. By the middle of the game, though, Mama was standing and cheering right alongside everybody else. Ben had bought Joseph a program and treated them to a hot dog and cola. Joseph used his own money to buy an American Giants pennant. Ben left them alone for a bit saying he had to go earn his keep and try to get some interviews for the newspaper. He rejoined them a short while later.

Willie Foster pitched an incredible game, leading the Chicago American Giants to win the series over the Bacharach Giants of Jersey City. Joseph felt a little guilty being in New Jersey and being so excited that the Chicago team had won. But he'd heard so much about Willie Foster.

As the crowd was filing out of the stadium, Ben told Joseph that he had a surprise for him. He and Mama followed him to a back door. Ben knocked on the door and in a low voice, said something to the man who opened it. The door was shut and Ben turned to Joseph.

"You better get your program handy. Here's a pencil."

"What are you talkin' about? What's goin' on?"

The door opened back up again. Two men stepped out and shook Ben's hand.

"Joseph, I'd like to introduce you to Willie Foster and his brother Rube. Rube was the founder of the Negro National League. They don't have much time but they'll sign your program, if you'd like."

Like? Of course he'd like. The problem was, his tongue was all tied up in knots and he couldn't say anything. The program was shaking in his hand, like the autumn leaves on the trees outside the stadium. The men gave Joseph big smiles, signed their names and handed the program back to him. He did manage to stutter out a thank you once Mama nudged her elbow into him.

***

The afternoon of October 9th, Joseph couldn't wait to get to his job at the newspaper. The night before, the New York Yankees became the hometown heroes by winning Major League Baseball's World Series. The city was going wild. Joseph wanted to hear what the reporters had to say about the game.

"So what do you think about the Yankees shuttin' out Pittsburgh, Joseph?"

"I knew they could do it. They got Babe Ruth!"

"After seein' the Chicago American Giants play, do ya think they could handle the Yankees?" Ben asked.

Joseph was beginning to feel like one of the guys when he hung around the reporters. This time, he answered with more confidence. "I sure do think they could handle the Yankees. I think they'd give 'em a real run for their money. You know what I'd like to see? Willie Foster pitch to Babe Ruth!"

The reporters all agreed with him. "What a game that would be," said Ben. "What a game!"

***

Not long after that, Joseph was at work when he heard about a tragedy that had struck the Harlem jazz community.

"Joseph, did you hear the news? Florence Mills died from an appendicitis attack." Ben shook his head sadly. "Folks in Harlem are busy planning a huge send-off for her. She made jazz famous from Harlem to Europe. We owe it to her."

On November 1st, the Harlem community turned out to remember Florence Mills in numbers never before seen. Five thousand people crowded Mother Zion AME church for her funeral. One hundred-fifty thousand people formed a funeral procession. Joseph stood on the side of the street, taking in all the sights and sounds. He remembered the night he sat on the front steps, thinking Harlem was a parade that was passing him by. Things sure had changed. But he wasn't going to let this real parade pass him by, either. He pulled his harmonica out of his pocket, stepped into the street, and marched and played along with "The Saints Go Marching In."

On the way home, after the procession, Joseph felt for the 1927 penny which Mr. Morgan had given him as change that first day of work. Every morning Joseph put it in his pocket, and every evening he took it out. He decided that it had given him so much good luck that it was time to share the luck. Every afternoon Joseph had passed a man who played his sax on the sidewalk. The man would have his case open next to him, hoping for people to put in spare change. Joseph often stopped to listen to the man play his music, but he had never put any money in his case. That particular afternoon, he listened to the man play a few songs. Then he walked up to him, tossed his penny into the case and continued on his way.

Chapter 7

PENNIES FROM HEAVEN

Maggie wondered why Billy always had to make things so difficult. He knew if the family couldn't agree on a movie to rent on a Friday night then they'd all have to play a board game together. She liked board games just fine, but Billy was a terrible loser. Plus, they'd have to agree on which game to play. Maggie thought they should buy the Family Feud board game; maybe they could all agree on that.

They were driving to the video store, on their way out for pizza. It was nice to be able to go out for dinner again. When Dad was out of a job last year, treats like this were the first to go. Now that he was back at work they could again get pizza and rent movies. Only now Billy found a problem with every movie suggested by someone else. Mom and Dad had a problem with the ratings of the movies he wanted to see.

"This is getting nowhere. Let's wait until we get to the store and look on the shelves; maybe there's a new movie out," Mom reasoned. "If not, then we'll just play a game."

It was a unanimous decision when they found out the latest King Kong movie had just been released. Family fun night was looking up: Pop's pizza and King Kong.

"You know, I've never seen the original King Kong," Mom commented. "I wonder if we could rent that. It might be fun to have a King Kong kind of weekend."

"I think it was made in the '30s. I'll see if they've put it on DVD." Dad went off to check with the store clerk and came back a few minutes later waving the movie triumphantly.

"It's not a silent movie, is it?" asked Tommy. "I don't think I could sit through a silent movie. Black and white is bad enough. The special effects have got to be weak."

"It's black and white, but it's what they used to call a 'talkie,' not a silent movie. I know we've been spoiled by special effects lately, but it'll be pretty funny to compare it to the new one." Dad paid for the movies and they headed back to the car.

Maggie's stomach rumbled at the thought of Pop's pizza. Usually they had pizza delivered on Friday nights, but tonight they were heading to their favorite pizza parlor. She loved everything about Pop's Place, from the enticing aroma when you walked in the door to the red-checkered tablecloths. Pop's had the best pizza in town. It was always crowded and everyone there seemed to be in a good mood. How could you not be? It wasn't exactly punishment to go to Pop's. Maggie smiled to herself as she imagined parents shaking their fingers at their kids and telling them that if they didn't shape up, they'd take them out to Pop's for pizza. There'd be an epidemic of kids getting into trouble.

After ordering their pizza, Mom and Dad started to quiz them about their days. As usual, when Billy was asked what he did that day he answered, "Nothing." Maggie pictured him at his desk all day, doing absolutely nothing.

"How come I never get Billy's teachers? I always end up with the ones that make us *do* something. How unfair."

"When you twins started school, we asked for you to always be in different classes. We didn't think to ask for Billy to be put in a class that *did* something." Mom smiled. "Okay, Maggie, tell us what you did today in your class that does things."

"We got a project assigned, but it's much better than the usual project. We have to look for the oldest penny we can find and then write about that year."

"That's pretty cool. I didn't get that project," complained Billy.

"That's what happens when you're in the class that doesn't do anything."

"Alright, we do plenty of stuff. I just don't feel like talking about it. But we didn't get a project like that."

"I guess they figured that since I was older, I was up to the challenge," teased Maggie.

"Older—not that again! Older by all of two minutes."

"I'll take what I can get," she laughed. "You know, I was just thinking it would be cool if I could find a penny from the 1930s—the time the first

King Kong came out. Do you think there are any pennies still around from then?"

"Maybe if you did a search on the Internet you could find out," Mom suggested. "You probably can buy all sorts of coins on there. If the price for a penny from the '30s isn't too expensive, then I would guess they're still in circulation."

"If they're cheap, why don't I just buy a penny from the year I want? That'd be easy."

"That seems a bit like cheating, doesn't it? Someone with the most money could just buy the oldest penny possible. I think that misses the point of the project. Your teacher probably wants you to go through the effort of looking for a penny. You can ask her on Monday."

Dad added his thoughts. "Other kids may have thought of that, too. If she doesn't want kids buying their pennies, she may want to have them sign an honor code about it. Someone else's mind may be as devious as yours, Maggie, but their parents may not be as hung up on ethics as we are."

"Life is so much harder when you have tough parents, isn't it?" laughed Mom.

"I'll probably have to look through a lot of pennies to find one from the '30s. If I do find out they're still around, where can I look for pennies?"

"You know, I think there was a song from the 1930s called 'Pennies from Heaven'," Dad said. "Maybe the penny you need will come down from above!"

"Why are you worrying so much about your homework on Friday night?" asked a bewildered Billy.

"I'm not worried about it. At least I think about my homework. It's not due for awhile, though. I have something else I have to do this weekend. I have to get pledges for the Drama Club fundraiser. We're trying to raise money so that we can take a bus to New York to see a Broadway play. We're doing something fun called 'moneylogues'."

"I've heard of monologues, but never a 'money-logue'. What's that all about?" Mom asked.

"Everyone in the Drama Club has to memorize and present a speech or monologue from a play. It has to be at least fifteen lines. We're actually going to recite them at the coffeehouse one night. We might get more donations there. I have to pick my monologue and get pledges this weekend."

"Why don't you ask people for pennies? Two projects for the price of one!" suggested Billy.

"You know, that's actually a good idea. I can't believe you came up with it. I want more than just pennies for pledges, though, or I don't think we'll end up paying for the trip. I could tell people that I'd accept pennies in their pledge. If I find an old one, I can just replace it with a different one. Thanks, Billy. I owe you one."

"And I won't let you forget it, either. Hey, our pizza's here!"

The table grew quiet as they all hungrily reached for a slice of hot pizza. Maggie bent her crust in the middle and touched the tip of the pizza to her lips. She knew if she took a bite now she'd burn the roof of her mouth with the hot cheese. She blew on the slice as she waited. She was experienced in being burned from impatience, so she counted to ten in her head. She started counting slowly, but by the time she got to seven she sped right to ten and took a bite of her pizza. Oh, it was so good. The crust was thin and chewy, but not too crispy, just the way she liked it. Pop's sauce was just the right spiciness and the cheese was warm and gooey. Pop's knew how to make pizza.

When they got home, Maggie checked the Internet for the prices of old pennies.

"There are pennies from the 1930s for only a dollar. There must be plenty of them around."

Billy was examining the two movies to compare their length. Since the evening was already getting on, they had decided to watch the shorter movie that night.

"Okay, the new King Kong is 187 minutes long." Billy announced.

"187 minutes! That's over three hours. How long is the old one?" asked Maggie.

"It's 95 minutes. I guess we'll be watching the old one. Darn!"

As they watched the movie, Maggie and Billy laughed and moaned at the lame attempts at special effects.

"This movie was made over seventy years ago. It came out during the Depression. It would have been a big deal to even buy a ticket to see the movie in

1933. A penny was worth a whole lot more then," Dad explained.

***

The next morning Maggie went through some of the play books she had brought home from school. She was hoping to impress everyone by reciting a Shakespeare monologue so that they might give her bigger pledges. They were filled with such strange words, though, that she wasn't sure she could memorize one. She decided to do one of her trusty Internet searches to find an interesting passage. Maybe that would be quicker. After reading, or trying to read, a number of monologues she was about to give up her Shakespeare idea. Then she came across a monologue that was actually given by a fairy. She didn't know Shakespeare had written about fairies. It came from the play *A Midsummer Night's Dream*. The verses even rhymed, making them much easier to memorize. She read some of the beginning lines aloud.

Over hill, over dale

Thorough bush, thorough brier,

Over park, over pale,

Thorough flood, thorough fire,

I do wander everywhere,

swifter than the moon's sphere;

And I serve the fairy queen,

To dew her orbs upon the green.

She decided that "thorough" must mean through; it made sense if she thought of it that way. She read the rest of the monologue to herself. The words were kind of fun to say; she might even like giving this speech. If she were feeling really theatrical she might dress in some kind of billowing fairy-like costume for the night at the coffee house. As long as Billy wasn't there.

After settling on the monologue, Maggie printed it to show the neighbors when she asked for pledges. It might help the cause. She got her pledge form and headed out the door.

The neighbors' enthusiasm was contagious. Not only did they write checks and give pennies, they all wanted to go to the night at the coffee house. She put the pennies in a bag, planning on looking over them as soon as she got home. She managed to memorize some of her lines as she went "thorough" the neighborhood. The lines kind of matched what she was doing. Between the first and second house she had memorized "over hill, over dale"—that was really easy, especially since she had to climb a steep driveway. Then after the next house she added "thorough bush, thorough brier," cutting through the bushes of the side yard. She took a turn through the neighborhood playground—"over park, over pale." What was a pale, anyway? She wondered if she had actually gone over one. She hoped the coincidences ended when she got to "thorough flood, thorough fire."

When Maggie returned home she felt like it was her lucky day. She had memorized some of her lines, gotten $125 in pledges and had a bag full of pennies. And it wasn't even Saturday afternoon yet. She went up to her room and sat cross-legged on her bed, dumping the pennies out in front of her. She wondered how many times somebody could have seen King Kong back in the '30s with all those pennies. She knew from the photograph on the Internet that she wanted a penny with a picture of wheat on the back. She focused her search on that. And then, it was as if the fairy queen herself had wandered everywhere, swifter than the moon's sphere, to dew her orbs, or in this case, her pennies.

For there, in Maggie's hand, was a penny from 1933.

Chapter 8

A PENNY FOR YOUR THOUGHTS

Maria sat on the curb with her mouth watering. She hadn't felt hungry, but the scent of Papa sizzling sausages and frying onions teased her taste buds to life. Papa's sidewalk grill was working its magic, luring customers who hadn't realized they were hungry, either. Maria could tell which way the spring breeze was blowing by whose nose was wrinkled up like a rabbit, while their head pivoted around looking for the source of the tantalizing smell. Maria breathed deeply, inhaling the aroma, knowing that alone would have to satisfy both her and many of the others walking by. She wouldn't be able to have a sausage because Papa needed to sell them. It was hard to believe that Papa used to have a busy restaurant where Maria could sneak pasta or bread and no one would mind.

But that was before the Depression. Papa's restaurant had to shut down; not enough people had money to spend in a restaurant. He was clever, though, and had come up with a way to make money to pay bills. He turned one of his old stoves from the restaurant into something he could use on the sidewalk to cook and sell sausages. Mama was a seamstress, and used to sew beautiful dresses during the Roaring Twenties. Lately, all she seemed to do was mend old clothes. Maria used to proudly wear new dresses made by Mama. Now, there wasn't enough money for new fabric. At least Mama knew how to alter Maria's old clothes so that she could still wear them as she grew.

"You're awfully quiet over there, Maria. A penny for your thoughts?" Papa's deep voice brought her out of her daydreams.

"Would you really give me a penny for my thoughts?"

"I had a good day yesterday. I can spare a penny." He took a penny out of his cash box and handed it to his daughter. "Now, *cara*, tell me what you were thinking about."

125

Maria was used to her father spicing his language with Italian words. She heard *cara* often; it meant dear. Papa said that just like his sausages, his language needed Italian seasoning.

Maria held the penny in her hand as she talked. "I was just thinking about how much things have changed in the past few years. That's probably what everybody is thinking, I guess. You probably didn't get your money's worth."

"Time spent with you is worth a lot more than a penny! Things have changed, that's for sure. But don't you feel something different in the air? It's called hope."

Papa was always dramatic when he spoke. Mama said it was *passione*; he was filled with emotions. He was born in America to parents who spoke only Italian at home. Even when he spoke English, he sounded like a *baritone*, his deep voice booming like an Italian opera singer.

Maria thought about what Papa said about hope and looked around her. It was an early spring day. There weren't any leaves on the trees yet, but the mid-morning air had the hint of warmth to come. People were walking outside on the sidewalk. After the long winter and the tough times, people were ready to be outside and feel hopeful. Everyone seemed to have a touch of spring fever.

"It *is* a beautiful day today. But is there something else that's making people feel hopeful? I've heard so many sad things as I've helped you with the stand, Papa, like about people, and even whole families who have had to live in cardboard shacks because they can't pay rent. I heard there are whole towns made up of these shacks. They're called 'Hoovervilles', after President Hoover. I also overheard one man say that homeless people call the newspapers they used to keep warm at night 'Hoover blankets'. Why did they name these things after our last president?"

"I see a customer heading this way. I'll explain it to you after I wait on him."

Maria sat down, watching the customer walk up to the sausage stand. He was a regular, lucky enough to have some money to satisfy the craving brought on from the scented smoke. She looked down at the penny in her hand. It was a 1933 penny—a new one from this year.

As the gentleman waited for his sausage, he struck up a conversation with Papa. "Have you been to see King Kong yet, Mr. D?" Everyone called Papa "Mr. D" because of their long last name. Papa's name was Anthony DiBenedetto. Papa would tell people that it was "Mr. D," just like the new president, Franklin D. Roosevelt.

"No, but my Maria keeps asking to see it. Have you been?"

"Yes, sir. It sure is something. A lot of folks are going to see it. I think with all the tough times they're happy to escape in a picture show for a little while. I guess it's like a ten-cent vacation."

After the customer left, Maria asked Papa a question. "Will I ever get to see King Kong? I want a ten-cent vacation!"

"Can you think of a way you can earn ten cents to pay for the movie? My sausage money is for rent and groceries, not hour-and-a-half vacations!"

"Well, if you ask me for my thoughts nine more times, then I can see King Kong," laughed Maria.

"Speaking of thoughts, what were we talking about? Oh yes. You wanted to know why people named the shantytowns and newspaper blankets after Herbert Hoover. Well, after the stock market crashed and The Depression began, people felt like their president wasn't doing anything to help them out. They lost faith in him, and as an insult they came up with terms like 'Hoovervilles' and 'Hoover blankets'," Papa explained.

"We have a new president now, though."

"We sure do. I think that's part of the reason for this feeling of hope that's in the air today. Franklin D. Roosevelt has promised to make big changes during his first hundred days in office. We're right in the middle of those hundred days right now. Roosevelt is calling it a New Deal. He says he's going to create government programs to get people back to work. That's giving people a lot of hope."

"I sure hope things change. It's so sad hearing people talk about children having to drop out of school so they can earn some money for their families. The other day, I saw another family's furniture and clothes out on the sidewalk. I heard they were kicked out of their apartment since they couldn't pay their rent." Maria looked down at the sidewalk. "Do you think there's any chance I could find any pennies on the sidewalk?"

"I don't think anyone would pass over a penny these days. You'll just have to figure out a way to earn the ticket money."

Maria could see that Papa wouldn't give her any money to see the movie. She went into the apartment building and up the three flights of stairs to talk to Mama, who was fixing an old wedding dress to fit a new bride.

"Mama, how can I earn ten cents to pay to see King Kong? Papa said I have to earn the money myself. Do you have any ideas?"

Mama looked up and took the pin out from between her lips. "While you've been with Papa, Anthony has been sitting in here pestering me. Maybe, if the two of you put your heads together, you can come up with something. If you can earn twenty cents, you can go see the movie together," she suggested.

Maria had imagined seeing King Kong with her friend June, not Anthony. Mama probably just wanted Maria to get him off her hands. She had no idea how they could even be related, let alone twins. Maybe they weren't. She had told him once that he'd really been born to another family that took one look and said they didn't want him. Mama had felt bad so she took him in, pretending the babies were twins. Maria had to admit they looked alike, with their olive complexion, dark hair and brown eyes.

"I really want to see King Kong. But where would we get any money? I hear there's money in bootlegging," Anthony joked.

Mama shook her finger at Anthony. "Don't be a smart aleck. Outlawing alcohol seemed like a good idea at the time, to a lot of people. Now there's just a lot of illegal money being made, with people flat out ignoring the law or sneaking around it. Instead of reducing crime, it seems to have made it worse. There's talk that Prohibition might even end this year. And, why are you still here pestering me? I've got sewing to do. Go on outside and think of a real way to earn your money for the cinema."

Maria and Anthony walked down the stairs. When they opened the door to the street, they were assaulted by the smell of Papa's sausages.

"I'll get too hungry if we stay here. Let's walk around the block," suggested Maria.

As they walked down the street they saw desperate men and women lining the sidewalks, selling apples for five cents apiece. Lots of the apples looked like they were going bad.

"I guess we won't be selling apples to earn ticket money," observed Anthony.

As they turned the corner, they saw Maria's friend, June, playing hopscotch on the sidewalk in front of her building. Her long blond braids bounced along with her.

"Hi, Maria. Hi, Tony Baloney! You wanna play?"

June always called him Tony Baloney instead of Anthony. That's what friends were for, she always said.

"If it isn't Loony Junie!" Anthony retorted. Oh well, that's what brothers were for.

"I was getting hot out here and just got some lemonade. Would you like some?"

"Sure. While we drink it, maybe you can help us with our problem. Mama and Papa said we have to earn our own money to see King Kong. I really want to see it, but I have no idea how to get the ten cents," lamented Maria.

A PENNY FOR YOUR THOUGHTS

"Oh, I want to see it, too. I saw the poster of the movie. I told my mother that I'd like to get my hair cut like Fay Wray!"

The three of them sat on the wall outside June's building, brainstorming their ideas. A flaw was found in every suggestion. Maria stared into her lemonade as she thought.

"I've got it! The idea is right in front of us. Why don't we open a lemonade stand?"

"How are we going to get the money to buy the lemonade ingredients and everything else?" Anthony asked.

"Our parents don't have a lot of extra money, but maybe they can lend us the money to get us started. We could pay them back before we take the money to see King Kong," June suggested.

Anthony looked doubtful. "I don't know if Mama and Papa would do that."

"When I was with Papa at his stand earlier, it was busier than usual. Maybe he has some money in his cash box to lend us. If we get started fast, we could set up next to his stand today. People might get thirsty from his sausages and buy lemonade from us!"

June got caught up in Maria's enthusiasm. "I'll see how my parents can help. You talk to your father. I'll meet you at the sausage stand as soon as I can."

As Maria and Anthony headed back to the stand, they worried that Papa would find some reason to dampen their excitement. Maria really wasn't sure he would lend them any money.

As they turned the corner, Maria saw there were several customers waiting for sausages. That was a good sign. She told Anthony they should wait until Papa was alone to ask him their question.

Papa was quiet as he thought about their proposal. Maria couldn't tell what was going on inside his head. She anxiously waited for his answer.

"I think that's a good idea. It's a chance for you two to get business heads on your shoulders. I'll be the bank, lending you money. I don't think it will take too much money to get started. I can also invest in your company by letting you use some of the restaurant supplies in the cellar. There's a table and three chairs you can use. And pitchers and glasses. I've also got some sugar put away which I'll sell to you, at cost. So, you'll only have to borrow money to pay for the sugar and lemons. You'll learn a lot from this with only a small investment from me."

Anthony and Maria shook hands as business partners. Maria hugged Papa in spite of his butcher's apron, which was smeared with grease from the sausage stand. "Thank you!"

"Now, I must get back to my sausages. I think you'll have a very good location next to my stand. If customers have enough money, they might buy lemonade to have with their sausage."

"Oh! What would people pay for a glass of lemonade? What should we charge?"

"Well, a sausage costs ten cents. They could get a soft drink at a counter for ten cents. I think you should charge less so they choose your lemonade. What about five cents a glass? It may take you a little longer to make your King Kong money, but at least you'll sell lemonade."

Right then, June came running down the street and screeched to a halt at the sausage stand. "My parents said they don't really have money to give to us. But my father said if we can start our lemonade business then he'll make a sign for us in his sign shop."

"Papa said he'd help us out! He'll lend us money for lemons and sugar and we can use his restaurant supplies."

"Thank you, Mr. D. My father said if he does make a sign he needs to know how much we're going to charge for a glass."

"Papa thought we should charge five cents. Why don't you go back and tell your father the cost? You can wait until the sign is ready and bring it back." Maria felt her entrepreneurial instincts kick in. "Anthony and I will get the other things together. When you come back we can go buy lemons and make the lemonade," she dictated.

"Who made you the boss? I want to make some decisions," Anthony complained.

"I'm not the boss. It's a three-way partnership. Come up with ideas!"

***

By the afternoon, the three were in business. June's father had made a very professional sign for them. After all their hard work, they were thirsty. Looking at the lemonade made them even thirstier. Anthony reached to pour himself a glass.

"Tony Baloney, we can't drink up all our profits!"

"Well, if we sit here drinking water, people will think our lemonade isn't very good," Anthony commented. "Why don't we pour one glass of lemonade and put three straws in it? We can share it. If we're still thirsty, we can take turns going inside for a drink of water."

"That's a good idea, Anthony. Maybe you'll turn out to be a good partner, after all."

Maria had another thought. "Why don't we give our 'banker' a glass of lemonade as a gift? If the glass of lemonade is sitting on Papa's stand, it might make people think of having a lemonade with their sausage."

It seemed that, as soon as the lemonade stand was set up, all of the sausage customers were gone. Papa told them that was how business was sometimes. They needed to be patient. While they waited for customers, Maria and June played some of the hand clapping games and songs that they had

137

learned from other girls at school. Anthony just looked up and down the street.

"Girls! Pay attention! Here come some people," Anthony ordered.

A man stopped at the sausage stand. Papa served the man his sausage then picked up his lemonade and took a sip. He winked at the children.

"It's a lovely warm day, isn't it, sir? A nice day for an outside lunch."

The children watched the man take a bite of his sausage. They saw Papa take another small sip of lemonade. The man was also watching Papa. "Where did you get the lemonade? I could use something to drink."

"I got it at the lemonade stand right next door. It's delicious and only five cents a glass."

"Let's see what I've got left in my pocket," the man said as he reached into his pants pocket. "I'm in luck. I have five pennies—enough to buy myself a lemonade."

June got the glass, Maria poured the lemonade and Anthony collected the money. The man drank his lemonade and left the glass on the table. Maria had brought up an old milk crate from the restaurant to hold the used glasses. They would wash them at the end of the day. The man told them that their lemonade was delicious and that he'd tell other people about their stand. Then he went on his way.

"*Congratulazioni*! You've had your first sale. Put your money in your cash box."

They sold a few more lemonades in the next few minutes and then had another quiet spell. Maria started thinking about business and money.

"Papa, now that I am a businesswoman, maybe I can understand if you explain about the Depression. I never did understand the stock market crash, the banks closing and all the people out of work. Would you try and explain it to us now?"

"I think I can explain it in a way you'll understand. We'll use your lemonade business as an example. Imagine you opened your lemonade stand a few years ago, when people had more money to spend. We'll say that you opened it well before the stock market crash."

Papa told them to imagine their lemonade stand with customers lined up. He told them to imagine they were making plenty of money to pay him back the start-up money, to buy more supplies, to go and see movies and still have money left over.

"What would you each do with the extra money that you would have?" Papa asked.

"I'd want a beautiful new dress, and if it wouldn't hurt Mama's feelings, I'd like to buy it from a store!"

"I'd buy some new chalk for hopscotch," June chimed in. "Then, if there was still money to spend, I'd buy some fancy new shoes. But I'm also hungry, so I think I'd buy a sausage from you, Mr. D!"

"Remember, we're imagining a few years ago, when times were good. You could have come into my restaurant to buy a meal," Papa laughed.

"I'd get baseball tickets!" Anthony announced.

"Now, let's imagine that business is so busy that lines are getting quite long. You decide you should open more lemonade stands and make even more money. The only problem is that you've been busy spending. You haven't saved enough of your profits yet to buy all the supplies and to pay employees before the new stands start making money. You have the idea that you could borrow some more money from the Bank of Mama and Papa."

Maria laughed. "The Bank of Mama and Papa! I like that. I've already been to that bank. The people who run it are very nice people."

"We'll see how you feel about that in a little while," Papa said mysteriously. "Let's get back to your growing business, though. You also decide to sell ownership shares in your new business, so that you don't have to borrow as much. Your friends and their parents agree to buy shares in your company. They became investors in your Lemonade Stand Company. You get money from them and they own a little part of your business, but the three of you are still in charge."

Anthony stood up tall. "I like being in charge."

"That may change soon, too. The plan with your investors is that if they ever want their money back, they'll be able to sell their shares to someone else. The idea is that your lemonade stands will be so successful that they can sell the shares for more money than they paid for them. Everyone is very excited about this."

"I'm very excited about this, too! Think of all the money! " June's eyes grew large.

"Well, money's important. You'll need some for all these big plans. So you set up an arrangement with the Bank of Mama and Papa that they'll give you some of their money as a loan, which in a regular bank would be the savings that other people have put in their bank accounts. You're actually using other people's savings. Did you know that's how banks work?"

"I just thought it was the bank's money. I never thought about where they got it from," admitted Maria.

"The bank charges you some money—called interest—for the privilege of borrowing from them. They pass along some of that interest money to the people who keep their savings in the bank. Those people had put their money in the bank to earn a little money and to keep it safe. That's how a bank works."

"Anyway, you get your money from the bank and your investors, open more stands, hire employees and business continues to boom. Now, you and your employees are making money. All of you are continuing to spend money on a nice lifestyle. Because more people are spending money on more products, more companies start to open. Do you understand all this so far, *bambine*?"

Anthony answered, "I don't know about the girls, but I do. I'm getting very excited thinking that maybe our lemonade business will turn out like that."

"Well, remember, we're talking about a few years ago. I'm giving you the background for the stock market crash and the banks closing. This story isn't all good news."

Maria and June looked up and down the street, with no customers in sight. They realized they were doing such a good job of imagining that they forgot what times were like now.

"First things first. Back to the boom times. People also see how successful your lemonade stand is, so they open up cookie stands. Some people even open up lemonade stands, trying to compete with your lemonade. You decide to lower your prices so people will buy your lemonade. Between the lower prices and the loss of some customers to other stands, you aren't making as much as you used to. A few of your investors decide this might be a good time to sell their shares in your business. But other people have also noticed the change in your business. They don't want to pay as much as your investors are asking for their shares. These investors sell for a lower price and lose some of their money. Other investors hear about it and start to panic. They try to sell their shares, but now more investors are trying to sell their shares than there are people who want to buy them. Therefore, buyers can haggle for a lower price. This keeps going until nobody wants to buy, and the shares have become worthless. All the investors have lost their money. For some of them, it was their entire life savings."

"I feel terrible. We were the cause of people losing their life savings. Things were going so well." Maria looked crestfallen.

"That's how a lot of people have felt, Maria. But don't feel too bad. We're only playing an imaginary game. You didn't cause anything to happen, my *tesorino*."

A young couple, holding hands, walked up to the sausage stand, ordering one sausage to share between them.

"Ah, *amore*! There's nothing like love in the springtime."

June leaned over and whispered to Maria. "Maybe they'll share a lemonade, too."

Maria whispered back, "Papa is a good businessman. We need to learn from him and be friendly, too." Then she spoke louder, to the couple at the sausage stand. "We can sell you one lemonade and give you two straws for free!"

Maria's sales pitch resulted in a sale and a chuckle from Papa. The couple walked down the sidewalk with their sausage and lemonade.

"Okay, Papa. Things weren't going well. What next?"

"Well, as your business was dropping, you were finding it hard to make your loan payments to the Bank of Mama and Papa and to pay your employees. You decided to pay your employees because you figured they were really counting on you. Unfortunately, you had an arrangement with the Bank that if you didn't make your loan payments the Bank could close your business. They could take your money and whatever supplies they could sell, in order to get back as much of their loan money as possible. Also, the Bank wanted something called 'collateral' when they first loaned you the money—something else they could sell if the sale of your used supplies didn't cover the loan."

"Papa, did you have to give collateral for your restaurant?" Anthony asked.

"I rented the building so I didn't have a loan on that. If I had, then the building would have been collateral on the loan. My restaurant equipment had been the collateral on the loans to buy them. But when times were good I had been able to pay back those loans. So when times got bad I just shut down the restaurant since I could see I wasn't making enough to pay the rent and other bills. But I was lucky; I didn't owe anyone money."

"But the timing was different for your business. You needed the money and were so sure that your business was going to last forever that you had given them the deed to your clubhouse. So, it ends up that you lost all of your investments as well as your clubhouse, the bank lost money on the loan because people didn't really want your used supplies and didn't have much money to buy a clubhouse, and your employees lost their jobs. Investors in other companies found out about your company's tragic story and started to worry. If it happened to your company, they realized it could happen to the one in which they had bought shares. So, they decided to sell the shares in the company they invested in—maybe it was the cookie stand or other lemonade stand. Again, more people wanted to sell than buy and a lot of people lost a lot of money. Everyone started to panic." He paused. "Do you need a break from this story?"

"The girls might, but I don't. I want to know what happens next."

"We do too," said Maria.

"Hold on just a minute. I see one of my regular customers walking down the street. I'll bet he's coming to buy a sausage. Maybe he'll buy a lemonade today, too."

That's exactly what happened. After that customer left, more came. A few bought only sausages, but most bought a lemonade as well.

When things got quiet, Papa continued his story. "Where were we?"

"Everybody was in a panic," Maria reminded him. "People were losing jobs and money."

"Okay. All these people who lost jobs needed some money to live on so they went to the Bank of Mama and Papa to withdraw their savings. Well, the Bank had loaned out a lot of their money, not expecting so many people to want to take out their savings at the same time. The Bank had lost a lot of that loan money as well. There wasn't enough money available to give the people what was rightfully their money. The Bank of Mama and Papa ran out of money and had to close. Because of all this chaos, a lot of people lost their jobs, their investments, their houses and their savings."

"That is so sad, Papa. Now I understand. That may have just been a story about our lemonade stand, but it makes sense. It just happened in a bigger way all over the place."

"That's right. But the story isn't really over. It's still going on. People are going through rough times, but they still have hope. They're willing to work hard to make things better. Hope is what gets us through times like this. President Roosevelt seems to really understand how much people need to feel hopeful about something."

"Papa, why's the new president supposed to be different?" asked Anthony.

"Well, he has a lot of changes in the works. President Hoover was convinced that the government should stay out of it. It's a tricky thing trying to figure out how much government should get involved. Things got so bad, though, that people felt something had to be done. Our new president is trying to get the economy moving in the right direction. He's planning on creating jobs that will make this country better. He's planning ways to make the stock market and banking safer for people."

"Will these times really come to an end?" asked Maria. "When will things be better, like they used to be?"

"I wish I could tell you when, but I do have faith that things will eventually get better. The president's plans have given me hope. It just may take time."

"I've done a lot of talking today, Maria. I think you should give me back that penny for all the thoughts I've given you!"

"I'm keeping that penny in my pocket. It has me filled with some hope," laughed Maria. "I'm hoping that we'll get to see King Kong!"

Chapter 9

COIN TOSS

James slid across the kitchen's wood floor in his white gym socks, coming to a stop right next to Mom at the counter.

"Thanks, the floor needed sweeping. Can you go around a few more times?" Mom reached over and tousled his hair. He shook it back into place.

"No, because then it would become a chore, instead of fun," he responded with a grin. "What's for dinner? Something smells good."

"Steaks are on the grill and potatoes are in the microwave. It won't be much longer. Snack on these carrot sticks. Do you have any homework?"

"Nothing due tomorrow. I have a project where I have to look through pennies for the oldest one I can find. Then I have to find stuff out about that year. But it's not due for awhile."

Mom turned up the volume on the small TV under the kitchen cabinets. James sat at the counter, mindlessly crunching on carrots.

The six o'clock news had just started. A picture of the smoking World Trade Center buildings was in the upper corner of the screen as the anchorman spoke. "As the war on terror continues, the American death toll in Iraq now exceeds the number of people that were killed in the attacks on September 11, 2001 . . ."

James spoke over the TV. "September 11 this, September 11 that. I'm so tired of hearing it all the time and them always showing that horrible picture. They totally wrecked my birthday. Whenever people find out when my birthday is, they always say something about 9/11. It's never just my birthday anymore."

"James, I know you're just a kid and birthdays are pretty special, but a lot more than your birthday was wrecked that horrible day. You still get presents and your whole family still sings happy birthday to you. There are a lot of kids who'll never have one or even both parents singing to them, because they were killed that day. You're old enough now to understand that. You know, when I grew up there were kids who had a birthday on December 7 and everyone would remind them it was the anniversary of Pearl Harbor. It really is important to remember the date and what happened. I'm lucky because unlike a lot of people, I also have wonderful memories associated with September 11. That will always be the day I gave birth to you."

James put his elbows on the counter and rested his chin in the palms of his hands. He heaved a sigh. "I know that. I guess it's just whenever I see that horrible picture it makes me kinda sick to my stomach. I was just a little kid when it happened, but I remember walking into the family room when you and Dad were watching TV that night. They were showing the airplane going into the building. It really scared me. It's like they keep trying to replay that scary feeling."

Mom set the dinner plates on the table, turned off the TV and sat next to James at the counter. "I remember waking up many mornings after that, remembering what happened and feeling like someone had punched me in the stomach. Where I grew up, I could see the Twin Towers being built. I remember going to the top of them on a field trip. When 9/11 happened, people I'd gone to school with were missing. It really was beyond belief. While it's a good thing that the feeling isn't as raw as it was then, we really do need to be reminded of it. It honors the memory of the people who died and reminds us to do everything in our power so it doesn't happen again. I'm so sorry that the images of that day had to be part of your childhood memories." Mom reached over and combed his hair with her fingers. Sometimes it annoyed him when she did that, but right now it felt pretty good.

"What they just said on the news is so confusing, too. Now more Americans have died fighting the war on terror than on 9/11. That doesn't make sense, does it?" James asked. "What's the point of that? How does it end?"

"I wish I knew the answer. This is so different from other wars we've been involved in. There are a lot of different opinions about it. I think we should read about the different opinions and the different options for dealing with the situation, and then sit down as a family and discuss them. It's important to understand all sides of the issue. You know, when I was in the airport last week a long line of soldiers marched by. Everyone stood up and applauded them. During the Vietnam War there were also a lot of strong feelings against the war, but sadly, they were taken out on the soldiers. People even spit at them when they came home. I was fighting back tears when these men and women were applauded, and I couldn't help wondering who would and who wouldn't make it back."

The microwave buzzer went off and Mom got up from the counter. James thought about what she'd said about the soldiers. They were just doing their jobs. Some of them might even be as confused as he was about the whole thing. He hoped this was all over before Jack was old enough to fight. He couldn't imagine what it would be like if his older brother ever went to war.

The door from the deck opened and Dad walked in carrying the steaks on a plate. He messed up James's hair as he passed by. What was it with his hair today? No one could keep their hands off it. He smoothed it back down again.

"What's up?" Dad asked as he reached for one of the carrot sticks.

"Well, Mom was just telling me how everybody clapped for the soldiers in the airport last week. Since I'm never in the airport to clap for them, I was wondering what I could do to show my support. Any ideas?"

"You can write letters or send care packages. I know they love to get stuff from home. Haven't you been putting off coming up with a service project for Scouts? Maybe you could do something with that."

Mom handed James the silverware to set the table. "You know, they're having that Fall Family Fun day at the park by the beach next weekend. Maybe you could get permission to set up a table to collect donations for care packages."

James began to place the silverware around the table. Did the spoons go on the inside or outside? Never mind, they could just fix it if they didn't like it. He got back to thinking about care packages.

"I could see if Scott wants to do it with me. He hasn't come up with a service project either. I'm sure our leader will approve it. We talked so much about pennies at school today—do you think we could collect enough pennies to pay for care pack-ages?"

Dad walked around the table, setting out napkins and changing the position of the spoons. "I think there's time to get a notice in the local paper. You might be surprised how quickly pennies add up. Maybe you could ask for all kinds of loose change so that it adds up to even more."

The side door opened and shut with a slam. Jack was home. Just in time, as usual. He had natural radar for dinner.

"What could I call the project? Wouldn't it be good to name it?"

"I don't know what project you're talking about, but why don't you name it after yourself, Lame James?" Jack playfully punched James in the arm. At least he didn't mess around with his hair, thought James.

"You are so funny. Do you think you're clever enough to come up with a real name for a fundrais-ing project I'm gonna do? I'm having people donate loose change so I can send care packages to sol-diers."

"Give me a minute. I know I can come up with something." Jack reached for a piece of scrap paper and a pencil. He started to scribble words down. He kept scribbling and scratching out.

"Okay, pick one. 'The Power of One,' 'Change is good,' or 'Common Cents.' What'll it be?"

"Not bad. I like them all. Write them each on a scrap and let me choose without looking." James closed his eyes and pulled a slip of paper out of Jack's hand. Then he opened his eyes to read his choice.

"'Common Cents' it is!"

***

James and Scott were able to get a notice in the paper and they posted signs around town as well. The day of the Fall Family Fun Day found them at a long table. They had made a banner to hang on the front of their table which said COMMON CENTS in huge block letters. In smaller letters they had written "care packages for the troops," "donate your loose change" and "send a note of thanks." People were lined up to drop their coins into the buckets.

The table was crowded with adults and children writing notes and coloring pictures.

"Scott, we need to look through these pennies when we get a chance. We might find some good ones for our social studies project."

"The oldest one in my mom's purse was from 1978. My parents said I should be excited to find that year, because it was historically significant." Scott smiled. "It's when they graduated from high school!"

"With all these pennies, you have to be able to do better than that. You don't want to have to bring their yearbook in as a prop. Think of those hairstyles!" James reached into the bucket and sifted out some pennies.

"2000, 1998, 1985 . . ." James continued reaching in for pennies and reading the dates aloud.

"How are we going to decide who gets to keep the oldest penny?" asked Scott.

"I know!" James laughed. "We'll toss a coin!"

The boys got tired of looking through pennies so they took turns going on breaks to eat the food at the festival and play games on the beach. At the end of the day they agreed they'd each take a bucket home. After they looked through them for old pennies, they'd go together to take them to the coin machine at the store. Then they'd shop for things for the care packages. They couldn't wait to find out how much money they raised.

It was late that night when James nearly fell out of bed, but it wasn't because he was sleeping. He was so tired that he thought he must have read the date on the penny wrong. He looked at it again, and then he looked at the clock. It was too late to call Scott. He ran to the computer to send him an email.

"Scott, you won't believe what I found. A penny from 1941!!!! Coin toss tomorrow." He clicked SEND. As his message was sent, he saw that he also had an incoming email from Scott. It read:

"James! You won't believe it. I found a penny from 1941!!!! Coin toss tomorrow."

Chapter 10

TWO CENTS' WORTH

Bobby sat on the beach, running the cool grains of sand between his fingers. He couldn't imagine living anywhere other than near the beach, even on a frosty December day. Just a few months back he had been hopping across the blazing hot sand, convinced that his feet were blistering from the burns. He remembered how good the cold water had felt on his feet. The chill of the water wouldn't be welcome on a day like today, though. Bobby took a last look out into the Atlantic. Dusk came early these days, so he knew he'd better walk home before he heard his mother's voice calling him. As he looked out to sea, he thought about the war in Europe. It was so peaceful here, sitting on the quiet beach at twilight. It was hard to believe that on the other side of the water a terrible war was taking place. He felt sorry for everyone over there, but was happy for all the water between Europe and the United States.

After supper, his parents turned on the radio to listen to the news. This was a nightly routine at his house. Bobby flopped onto the living room floor with his bucket of dime-store soldiers. His older brother, Charlie, had taken a date to the movies. She had pleaded with Charlie to take her to see the new Disney film, *Dumbo*.

Bobby didn't really pay attention to the radio as the reporter gave updates on local news, politics and the economy. As he finished lining up his soldiers into neat rows, along the gold stripes on the burgundy rug, he realized the report had moved onto the war in Europe. He started to pay attention since his toy soldiers were divided into English, Russian, Italian and German battalions. The English and Russians were fighting against the Germans and Italians to keep their territory to the left of the coffee table. Bobby called a temporary truce as he listened to the broadcast.

The static-filled radio droned on in its monotonous outpouring of information. ". . . Soviet forces attacked German lines around Moscow. Fresh and well-equipped Soviet forces from Siberia and the Far East were supported by new tanks and rocket launchers. Word is that these Soviet troops are prepared for winter battle, even having battalions of troops on skis . . ."

Bobby rearranged his rug warriors. The English soldiers became the ski battalions of the Soviet army. The Italians and Germans became one large German army in Moscow. The area to the left of the coffee table became Moscow. The news finished and as music began to play his parents discussed what they'd heard on the radio. Dad seemed to be upset with the news.

"I really don't know how long we're going to be able to have limited involvement in this conflict. Not much more than a month ago we had another destroyer torpedoed and damaged off Greenland, and then another sunk off the coast of Iceland. In November, we gave a huge loan to the Soviet Union. Maybe it was that loan that made this latest attack possible. I just see this continuing to spiral out of control. I hope I'm wrong."

"Well, I do too. I can't stand to think of any more boys from the naval base having to be sent out on patrol. It seems country after country has been dragged into the war. It's covering Europe, the Middle East, Africa, and the Pacific." Mom was knitting so aggressively, it seemed the needles were fighting their own battle.

"The powers of Germany, Italy and Japan have to be stopped in some way. I don't see how much longer it can go on like this."

"Dad, I always hear talk about the Axis Powers and the Allied Forces. I know we're on the side of the Allied Forces, but what do their names mean?" Bobby could count on Dad knowing the answer since he was a history professor at Rhode Island State College. Sometimes Bobby didn't even ask questions because he usually got more of an answer than he wanted. But he had to admit, Dad knew his stuff.

"Well, in 1936 Italy and Germany got together and signed an agreement to stand together, which was called 'The Rome-Berlin Axis.' That started the use of the term 'Axis.' That same year, Germany and Japan also signed an agreement. Two years ago, in 1939, Italy and Germany signed a stronger agreement with a name that was meant to intimidate the rest of the world: 'Pact of Steel.' In 1940, the three countries of Germany, Italy and Japan signed a pact together. Later, they were joined by Hungary, Bulgaria, Croatia and Slovakia. All those countries are now referred to as the Axis Powers."

Bobby could picture Dad at the chalkboard in class, furiously writing notes as he spoke. Maybe they needed a chalkboard in the living room. But Bobby had been paying attention and even without notes something clicked.

"I think I know why the other side is called the Allied Forces. An ally is a friend. The other countries sort of became friends together to fight the enemy."

"Exactly right! Have you been sneaking into classes at the college?"

Mom stood up and turned off the radio. "Time to clean up the troops and get to bed."

"Can't I leave them set up the way they are? Tomorrow is Sunday so I can play with them."

"After church one of the young men, John Roberts, from the college, will be joining us for Sunday dinner. You won't have a chance to play with them until after that."

"Hey! His last name is like my full first name. If I were in his family, I would be Robert Roberts!"

"Well, the last I checked you're still in this family. I'm still your mother and can make you clean up and go to bed."

***

The next day during church, Bobby's stomach started growling as he thought about the meal they'd soon be having. Mom always made a special meal when college students came over. They missed home-cooked meals so she tried to treat them as their mother might. He knew the house was probably filled with the smell of the roast beef in the oven. When they got home his mother would make her creamy mashed potatoes. She'd already made an apple pie for dessert. He really tried to pay attention to the minister but his mind kept wandering to his stomach. Finally, they bowed their heads for a closing prayer for peace. They wouldn't realize until later that day exactly how much that prayer was needed.

Bobby thought *he'd* been hungry, but he watched in amazement as John heaped huge seconds onto his plate. Bobby knew how happy that would make Mom. John might even write home about the nice lady who gave him a home-cooked meal. That would probably make John's own mother happy.

"This is delicious, ma'am. I haven't had a meal like this since I was home. We don't eat like this in the dining hall. Maybe you could give them a few tips."

"Somehow, I don't think trying to fill the stomachs of a dining hall full of hungry young people is the same as feeding four men," she laughed.

Bobby liked being referred to as a man. He'd been feeling like a little kid since Charlie was in high school and John was in college. He'd been listening to the conversation between Charlie and John, rather than doing much talking. He decided to ask John the kind of question a man might ask.

"John, do you think that President Roosevelt is going to have us get more involved with the war in Europe?

"I think he's trying as hard as he can to keep us out of the action. But, if things keep going like they have been, it's going to be hard not to get involved."

After the apple pie was cleared from the table, John announced that he needed to get back to his room so that he could do the homework his tough history professor had assigned. He smiled at Dad as he said it.

Once John left, the family gathered in the living room. Bobby was setting his Soviet/German soldiers back on the rug. Dad turned on the radio since it was nearly time for the weekly news program, *The World Today*.

Bobby had no idea that the news he was about to hear would make this a day he'd never forget for the rest of his life. He and his family listened in shock as they heard that an hour earlier Japanese planes had bombed the U.S. Naval base at Pearl Harbor, in Hawaii.

Dad was the first to speak, his voice strained with emotion. "I was so afraid something like this was going to happen. Now, we'll have no choice but to send our boys to war."

Bobby looked at Mom. Her shoulders were shaking as she sat with her face in her hands.

Charlie moved to sit right next to the radio, as if sitting closer would get him closer to the action.

Bobby thought about how Mom had just called them men. But now Dad had called them boys. When you thought about it, he reasoned to himself, the ones who lost their lives in Europe and now at Pearl Harbor really were still just boys. Especially to their parents.

That night at supper, Bobby sat with his family around the kitchen table listening to the radio's continuing broadcasts. They'd spent the day glued to the radio. As painful as the news was to hear, they couldn't stop themselves from listening. They'd learned that President Roosevelt was dictating a message to Congress and would probably declare war the next day. Japan announced it had entered a state of war with Britain and the U.S. The Secretary of State ordered that all factories and plants working on defense orders institute a guard against sabotage.

At 6:30 that evening, an announcement came over the radio. Nearby Quonset Naval Air Base ordered all Marines to return to their stations. Mom and Dad spoke of those they knew that were stationed in Honolulu and elsewhere in the Pacific, and worried for their safety. Bobby couldn't believe this was all happening. It reminded him of the *War of the Worlds* radio broadcast by Orson Welles a few years ago. It had been a radio show of the book, *War of the Worlds*, but people who had started listening in the middle of the show thought it was a real invasion by aliens. People everywhere panicked. That was just a pretend science fiction story though, and this was real.

The news broadcast announced that all military recruiting stations would be open the next day. Charlie jumped up from his seat.

"That's it! I'm going there tomorrow! I'm joining the Marines," he announced, as much to himself as to his parents and brother. "I'm not just sitting in some classroom while we're being attacked. I'm going to help defend this country."

"Charles! Don't be ridiculous. You're in your last year of high school. It's not the time to make an impulsive decision. We're all upset and need to wait until we have more information." Mom's voice was trembling.

"But I'm seventeen years old!" Charlie stood up and pushed his chair in so hard that the whole table shook. "The Navy lowered their enlistment age to seventeen this year. I can enlist and finish high school later."

Bobby felt like he was in a bad dream. He was on the sidelines watching everything fall apart around him. Charlie drop out of school? Fight in a war! This wasn't toy soldiers on the carpet anymore. This was real and he didn't like it.

"Dad, don't let Charlie enlist. Please don't let him!"

"Bobby, seventeen-year-olds can't enlist without the consent of their parents. Last year all men between the ages of twenty-one and thirty-six registered for the draft. They'll be called up as needed. Listen, Charlie. You can do your part now by completing your education. Let's wait and see what happens. We're all upset. I'm proud of you, though, for being willing to fight for freedom."

Charlie slumped back down, defeated, into his seat. Bobby wanted to race to his favorite spot on the beach, but it was too dark now. He thought about John Roberts and wondered what would happen to him. He stayed up late, listening to the radio with his family. At 10 p.m., a news broadcast announced that Canada had declared war on Japan.

"Dad, Japan attacked an American base. How come Canada declared war before we did?"

"In the United States, it takes an act of Congress to declare war. It's Sunday, but President Roosevelt has already written his letter to Congress. As soon as Congress can meet they'll declare war. Canada doesn't have to go through that process, and based on what happened to us, they see Japan as a threat. So, they declared war."

The next day, as expected, the United States and England declared war against Japan. In President Roosevelt's speech he said that December 7, 1941 was "a date which will live in infamy." Bobby remembered learning how the word "famous" was different from "infamous." He knew the President meant that the day would always be remembered for bad reasons. In Hawaii, the day before, the Japanese had killed many more people than had been first estimated. Over two thousand military personnel were killed and over one thousand were injured. Sixty-eight civilians were killed with dozens wounded. More than twelve warships had been destroyed or severely damaged, as well as 188 planes destroyed and 155 damaged.

Monday night at supper, the family talked about the news and what everyone else was saying about it. It seemed like a lot of Charlie's friends had similar conversations with their parents the night before. Dad said that a lot of the boys at the college were talking about enlisting. He tried to advise them not to make hasty decisions; they needed to wait and see how this played out for awhile. Bobby was disappointed to hear that John Roberts was from a Navy family and was one of the most outspoken students that day.

The following afternoon, Bobby looked at the clock in the classroom to see that only five minutes had gone by since he had last looked. It was 1:25 p.m. and he had been counting the minutes all day. Suddenly, sirens started blaring outside. Fire engines and police cars were going by, sounding their sirens. The sounds seemed to come from everywhere. Bobby and his classmates rushed to the windows to see what was going on.

"Class, back in your seats. I'll try to find out what's going on. Stay in your seats. I won't be long."

As the teacher left the classroom, the students returned to their seats. The wailing sirens continued outside the room while a buzz of conversation went on among the students. What was going on? Had they been attacked? Was the war *here* now? Bobby's stomach was in knots by the time his teacher came back.

"Children, school is being dismissed for the day. You'll need to go directly home. There was a report of enemy aircraft off the East Coast. Please stay calm, get your coats, and line up at the door. We'll all walk outside together."

It wasn't easy to stay calm. Bobby ran home, hoping Mom and the radio could tell him more. Mom was waiting on the front steps for him. She said that everything seemed to be okay. It might even have been a false alarm, but everyone had been instructed to keep their shades drawn at night so that they wouldn't be visible if enemy aircraft did approach the coastline. It wasn't long before

Charlie and his father were home as well. Everyone was shaken up from the incident.

Dad told them that John Roberts was indeed enlisting in the Navy. His father had been in the Navy and his family supported his decision. He would be training at the Naval Air Base nearby. Dad also told Charlie that there was an excellent way for him to take part in the war effort and still finish high school. He could be part of the Civilian Defense to scan the coastline for enemy aircraft. He would attend classes to learn his responsibilities.

"Can't I do it too?" Bobby knew he'd be good at it since he loved to sit on the beach and look out at the ocean.

"I'm sure you can be Charlie's assistant. The more eyes looking out, the better."

That night Bobby emptied his pockets before getting ready for bed. He emptied some coins from his pocket onto his desk. He had been planning to stop with some friends at The Candy Box after school. Instead, when those sirens went off he had rushed straight home.

He couldn't stop thinking about John Roberts, wondering where he'd end up being stationed after training. Mom had suggested he write him a letter to wish him good luck. As he sat at his desk thinking of what to say, he picked up a couple of the pennies that had been in his pocket. He looked at them and realized that they were both pennies from 1941. The pennies gave him an idea.

In the letter, Bobby told John that he'd be keeping a 1941 penny in his pocket every day. Every time he put his hand in his pocket and felt the penny, he'd think of John. He'd put the other penny in the envelope. He asked John to try to take his penny with him if he could, maybe in some pocket of his uniform. Then whenever he felt it, he could remember that Bobby was thinking of him and hoping he was safe. He told him he would look out at the ocean from his favorite spot on the beach and imagine where John's ship might be sailing. The 1941 pennies could remind them of the attack on Pearl Harbor and why John joined the Navy.

A couple weeks later, Bobby sat down for an after school snack of milk and homemade cookies. Mom had been making these since she had tasted them at the famous Toll House restaurant. Now they were so famous that the recipe was even on the bag of chocolate chips from the store.

He noticed a letter was propped up against the glass of milk. It was addressed to him! Even before taking a cookie, he tore the envelope and began to read.

Dear Bobby,

Thanks so much for your letter. I've been real busy training. How's your family? I do miss your dad's history classes. But, don't let him know I said that! I also miss your Mom's cooking and please do let her know I said that! Say hello to Charlie.

I really liked getting the penny with your letter. My uniform has the perfect pocket for it. I keep it safely buttoned inside. Through the penny's travels, you can travel along with me. I'll try to write now and then to give you updates on where the penny and I have been (if I'm allowed to say).

Keep your penny safe. I've got big plans for our pennies. When I get back home, I'm going to take you out for ice cream. We'll take our pennies out of our pockets and put them on the counter. I'll pay the difference. Then, we'll walk to the beach, sit at your favorite spot and I'll tell you all about how I helped the United States end the war.

Your friend,

John

Chapter 11

PRESENT YOUR PENNY DAY

The classroom wasn't large enough for the presentation, so Ms. Maxwell's class had taken over the multipurpose room for the day. Chairs were set up for the students and guests. Tables lined the side of the room and were laden with foods that had been popular in the years of the pennies. The principal and staff were going to be coming in and out during the day. Amelia whispered to Maggie that they were only coming in because food was being served. Some students were dressed in period clothing from the era of their project; others had bags of props with them. Ms. Maxwell clapped her hands in the familiar rhythm that was her sign for everyone to get quiet.

"Let's get started. This is going to be so much fun. I can't wait to see what everyone has to share. I happen to be in on a few secrets so I know everyone is in store for a special day. We'll start with the more recent years and work our way backwards to the years of the oldest pennies."

Amelia didn't usually like presentations, but she was excited about this one. She had a surprise for the class. But she had found the next-to-oldest penny in the class so she had to wait awhile. She settled in to watch everyone else present their projects.

Jay would be the very last presentation, so he was able to take pictures for the school newspaper. He was even hoping he might get one published in the town's local paper. He and Michael had a plan. Michael would write an article about the day and Jay would take a picture to go along with it. They'd submit them to the town paper. Just maybe they'd get published.

Maggie figured it'd be awhile before they got to 1933. She had to phone Mom about a half hour before her presentation. She wasn't allowed to use her cell phone, so she'd have to leave the room to use the office phone.

There were quite a few pennies from the 1950s and 1960s. There was some great food kids had brought in that would have been popular during their year. James and Scott still had their mouths full of Jell-O when Ms. Maxwell said they'd be next.

Scott was dressed in a very baggy Navy uniform. James was dressed in regular clothes but had a large bag with him. First, they told the class about their fundraising project to raise pennies for care packages for the troops in Iraq and how they both ended up with pennies from 1941. They each presented their research on important events of that year. After that, Scott stepped forward in his naval uniform. The flash from Jay's camera went off. Scott told everyone about his trip to his cousins' house over Thanksgiving.

"The year 1941 gave us a lot to talk about at the dinner table," he began. "My grandfather was in the Navy in World War II. This was his uniform. He had been in college when the Japanese attacked Pearl Harbor. He decided to quit college and enlist in the Navy. He served several years in the Pacific during World War II. He shared a lot of stories and also let me borrow some pictures. I wrote down his stories and put them along with the pictures into this scrapbook. I thought I could pass it around the classroom today. I'm going to surprise him with it as a Christmas present."

"My grandfather did come back from the war and he enrolled again in college. His tuition was paid for by the GI Bill, which President Roosevelt enacted in June 1944. My grandfather said that it had a huge impact on college enrollment. So many men and women went to college on the GI Bill after World War II that temporary housing had to be built at colleges. Junior colleges were started. My grandfather also said that the GI bill made a big difference in a college education being available to everyone, instead of just the elite rich. The GI Bill is still available, so soldiers coming back from the Middle East could go to college on it." As he concluded his speech Scott passed around the scrapbook he had made.

James stepped forward with his bag. "I also had connections to 1941 at my Thanksgiving table. "My grandfather and his brother came over to our house. They brought me something of theirs from 1941."

James reached into his bag and pulled out some binoculars which he put around his neck. "My great-uncle Charlie had wanted to quit high school and serve in the Marines after the attack on Pearl Harbor. His father had been a college professor, so education was very important to him. He and my great-grandmother did not want Charlie to quit school. They found out about a program for civilians that he could help out with. It was called the Civilian Defense. He was trained to identify enemy aircraft and volunteered by sitting on the beach, observing the sky. His younger brother, my grandfather, helped him with it. These binoculars are the actual ones that my grandfather and his brother used in the Civilian Defense during World War II." James paused for effect. The class was completely quiet as they digested everything that James had said.

James posed with his binoculars for Jay's camera. He then pulled something else out of the bag. It appeared to be a window shade.

"This is an example of something that also played an important part in security during the war. My grandfather said that he was our age when Pearl

Harbor was attacked. In addition to helping his big brother look for enemy aircraft, he had the daily job of pulling down the window shades. They were required to pull down the shades every night to keep the area dark in case enemy aircraft approached. He said there was actually a person who went door to door in the evening making sure everyone's shades were drawn."

"After Uncle Charlie finished high school, he did enlist in the Navy. My grandfather said it was a terrible time with his brother fighting in the war. Many of his friends from school had brothers who died in the war. Since my great-uncle was at our house for Thanksgiving, obviously he made it home. He also went to college on the GI Bill, graduating from the college where his father was a professor. I've brought my grandfather's favorite cookie from when he was a boy. Today we call them chocolate chip cookies."

When the applause for James and Scott's presentation settled down, Ms. Maxwell called Maggie to the front of the classroom. She told the class about the rough times in 1933. She explained the events that led to the Great Depression and how people lived. She then in turn shared a story from her Thanksgiving table.

"My great-aunt June came to our house for Thanksgiving. She told us about how she was our age during the Depression. She said that she really hadn't understood what caused all the problems until her friend Maria's father taught them a great lesson. He had owned an Italian restaurant before the Depression, but he had to close it. He paid his bills by selling sausages on the street. He taught them all about the stock market crash and the bank failures through a lemonade stand they ran next to his sausage stand. Aunt June said when things picked back up, her friend's father opened his Italian restaurant again. Maria's father became my Aunt June's father-in-law when she married Maria's brother Anthony. She said when she was our age she would never believe anyone if they had told her she'd end up marrying "Tony Baloney"! Maria and Anthony later took over the restaurant. Maria sold it after Uncle Anthony passed away. I think you might all know the restaurant. It's Pop's Place."

Maggie walked to the door of the classroom. Ms. Maxwell didn't seem at all surprised so she must have been in on it. Maggie opened the door and in walked her mother, carrying four boxes of pizza from Pop's Place. Everyone in the class let out a cheer. Maggie went to the back of the classroom and got a large jug of lemonade she had hidden back there. Three of the pizzas were plain cheese, but for old time's sake, one was Italian sausage.

It was time for Michael to give his presentation. He had become so absorbed in everyone's stories that the time had flown by. He'd been taking notes for the school newspaper article and the one he was going to submit to the local paper. He'd managed to get greasy sausage stains all over his notes. He wiped his hands on his jeans and went to the front of the room.

"My penny was from 1927. The 1920s are often called 'The Roaring Twenties' because they were known as such a prosperous time when people were really enjoying life. 1927 was before the stock market crash that Maggie talked about. No one knew what was about to happen. But, there were plenty of people who didn't have a lot of money during the 1920s."

He went on to explain about jazz music and its popularity during the '20s. He then told the class about his Thanksgiving experience. "My grandfather was at our house. I had already told him about my project so he came over prepared to share some stories. He told me that he had been born in 1927, in Harlem, New York. Of course, he doesn't remember anything from 1927 but he had an older cousin who used to tell him stories. He said his aunt and cousin lived with his family when he was born. His cousin Joseph was around our age in 1927. He worked part-time at a black newspaper in Harlem. His mother actually married a man named Ben that Joseph met at work. Joseph went on to a career in journalism. He became a newspaper editor.

"My grandfather asked me to play my saxophone for him. He said they used to hear the sax being played a lot in Harlem. After I played it for awhile, he told me that he had a present for me. He said since I really researched the 1920s and appreciated music, he wanted me to have something that was very special to him. It had belonged to his cousin Joseph." Michael reached into his pocket and set

187

the gift on the table in front of him. It was a well-worn harmonica.

Finally it was Amelia's turn. She looked at the clock and saw that she was right on schedule for her surprise.

She told the class all about the events of 1918. She explained how World War I was called The Great War and all about the influenza outbreak. She said how it was often referenced in current news about the fear of things like SARS, avian flu and other potential epidemics. The Center for Disease Control had researched a lot from that tragedy in hopes of preventing something like that from happening again. She then talked about her Thanksgiving trip.

"I went to Pennsylvania to celebrate Thanksgiving and my great-grandmother's 100th birthday. I call her 'GG' for short. GG is an amazing lady. I found out she was exactly our age in 1918. She shared a lot of stories with me and my family over Thanksgiving. One thing she remembered from her birthday that year was the gift a friend gave her—a jump rope."

At that point, Amelia pulled a jump rope out of a bag, and started jumping. She was known for her amazing jump rope skills; she was even on a competitive jump rope team. Jay's camera flashed again.

"GG remembered this jump rope song that her friend had taught her on her birthday:"

I had a bird

and his name was Enza . . .

Right then, Maggie went over and lifted the window. An elderly lady's head poked inside and recited,

I opened the window and

In-flu-enza!

The whole class burst out laughing. Jay took a picture of the smiling old woman, with her head in the window.

A few moments later the old woman came in the classroom door accompanied by Amelia's parents. She went to the front of the classroom and stood next to Amelia. Amelia introduced her.

"This is GG, my great-grandmother. Everyone else calls her Miss Penny. She came back from Pennsylvania with us after Thanksgiving."

"I'd love to answer any questions you might
have about my childhood experiences in 1918. That
is, I'll answer them if I can remember what happened," laughed Miss Penny. "But first, I have my
own surprise. Amelia doesn't know anything about
it. Because of your project, I thought you might *all*
enjoy my surprise."

Amelia's parents were in the back of the classroom with their camera and video camera. Amelia
looked completely perplexed.

"Amelia, I have decided that rather than wait for
you to receive this surprise when I'm gone and
can't see your face, I'd like to do it now."

She then handed her great-granddaughter a
wooden box. Amelia opened it, and for once she
was speechless. Tears filled her eyes as she hugged
her great-grandmother. Amelia turned the box to the
class, showing them her great-grandmother's penny
collection.

When Amelia couldn't speak, her great-
grandmother did.

"This box has been missing something since
1918. I think you have something that will make it
complete."

Amelia then looked for the empty space and, to a standing ovation from everyone in the room, added her 1918 penny to make it a complete collection.

The class took a break after Amelia's presentation. Everyone wanted to meet Miss Penny and see the penny collection. Some students even wanted Miss Penny's autograph. Everyone was chattering about the presentations, the stories and food. Finally, Ms. Maxwell's familiar clapping quieted them all down.

"What a day this has been! Soon it will be just a memory, like all these other memories we've heard today. Now it's time for our final presentation. Let's give Jay a round of applause for finding our oldest penny—from 1909!"

Jay walked to the front of the room, with the familiar camera around his neck and another small black box. He took the camera from around his neck and placed it on the table next to the box.

"Since I like photography, I wanted to show you the difference between the digital camera I use and what was used in 1909." He unhooked the black box and pulled out the accordion-type lens. "This was a foldable Brownie camera. It was quite a big deal when the Eastman Kodak company released it in 1909."

"Those are the only props I have and they both came from stores. My talk won't be as exciting as everyone else's. I'm just going to read my essay. I hope you don't find it too boring, especially after all the fun we've had. I don't have any family props from 1909. In fact, I don't even have any family that was here in 1909."

"I think it's funny that I found the oldest penny. Actually, Ms. Maxwell said the word for it was ironic. I could have found a penny from 1995 and I still wouldn't have any relatives that had been here to tell me their American experiences. I have no family history from the United States at all. Sometimes that's made me feel really left out. But I think I found the 1909 penny for a reason. I researched the year and learned all about the waves of immigration into the United States. When I learned about Hull House and all of its work for immigrants, I decided to focus my research on Chicago in 1909. People talk today about how different ethnic groups stick together, and if they're newer immigrants, how they talk in their native language to each other.

Some people feel that they aren't trying to fit in. Well, the same thing was said about one hundred years ago when cities had completely ethnic neighborhoods. Greek immigrants lived, shopped and went to church with other Greeks. They usually spoke Greek to each other. Italians, Germans, the Polish—they all did the same thing. Everyone wants to have a history to talk about. These people's history was in another country, just like my family."

"But more importantly, everyone wants to have a bright future. That's why those people immigrated in 1909. And now, almost one hundred years later, their children, grandchildren and great-grandchildren have an American history. Just like my children, grandchildren, and great-grandchildren will, too."

"Actually, I do have another prop and I'm going to ask her to come up now."

Jay's mother looked embarrassed as she walked up to the front of the classroom. She was wearing a beautiful pink *sari*.

"This is my mom. Just like me, she's an immigrant. She still prepares Indian food for our meals. She and my dad often speak Hindi at home and to their friends. She wears a *sari* for special occasions. She still clings to familiar and comfortable ways. But that's because she did the most unfamiliar and uncomfortable thing. She and my father moved to another country so their son could one day have an American history. I'm keeping my 1909 penny in my pocket so that I never forget what they did for me and what your ancestors did for *all* of us."

Everyone in the room rose to their feet; the adults clapped enthusiastically as the students waved their pennies in the air and cheered.

GLOSSARY OF PENNY EXPRESSIONS

The title of each chapter uses an expression, or idiom, about pennies or coins. An idiom is a phrase that is used with a different meaning than the words themselves express. Interestingly, when someone comes up with a unique phrase or idiom, it is called "coining a phrase"! Following is an explanation of both the literal meaning (the origin of the expression) and the figurative meaning (how it is used today and what it is generally understood to mean).

1. **THE PENNY DROPPED** – This phrase came about as a result of literally dropping a penny into a machine for a candy or other item, with the candy being released a moment later. When it is used today, it means that someone has been told something that takes them a moment to understand. When they do understand, then it is said that "the penny dropped."

2. **A PENNY SAVED IS A PENNY EARNED** – The meaning of this expression is straightforward: if someone saved their pennies, they would add up. Nowadays, the word "penny" is still used, but the meaning of the expression has expanded to include larger denominations of money. The idea is that you'd be surprised at how much more money you would have if you didn't keep spending small amounts, because those small amounts really add up over time.

3. **SEE A PENNY, PICK IT UP** – This is part of the expression "See a penny, pick it up; all day long you'll have good luck." One theory is that it was originally "see a pin, pick it up" and came about

during pagan times when a pin was used in casting a spell. By 1900 the word "penny" had replaced "pin." Although a penny certainly isn't as valuable now as it was back then, it is still considered good luck to find a penny. Some people believe it is the "heads-up" penny that is good luck.

4. **PRETTY PENNY** – This idiom may date back to the 1700s. It refers to something being expensive, as in: "That coat cost a pretty penny."

5. **IN FOR A PENNY, IN FOR A POUND** – The pound in this idiom refers to the British monetary unit, the pound sterling. The expression generally was applied to gambling or illegal activities. The idea behind it was that as long as the punishments were the same if you got caught, you may as well take a big risk and go for the big reward. Its current figurative meaning is that if you're going to try doing something in the first place, you may as well try your hardest and go all out to reap the biggest reward.

6. **LUCKY PENNY** – This probably is derived from the expression discussed above, "See a penny, pick it up, all day long, you'll have good luck."

7. **PENNIES FROM HEAVEN** – This expression first appeared as a movie title in 1936 and then as a popular song recorded by Billie Holiday. It has often been used as the title of movies and television shows. The words to the song refer to not worrying about storm clouds and thunder because during the storm there'll be pennies from heaven. Its meaning is similar to the expression "every cloud has a silver

lining" in that you can often find good when something bad happens.

8.   **A PENNY FOR YOUR THOUGHTS** – This expression originated in the late 1800s, during which time a penny postcard was introduced. The idea evolved that for a penny someone could write their thoughts to someone else. Nowadays it is used figuratively when someone is being very quiet and a companion would like to know what they're thinking.

9.   **COIN TOSS** – Coin tossing was a common game in ancient Rome. The game was called *navia aut caput* which meant "ship or head" since some of their coins had a ship on one side and a picture of a head of the emperor on the other side. The expression "heads or tails" came about because the coins of most countries had a picture of a head of state on one side. The opposite side was referred to as the tail. Coin tossing is used to this day to settle a dispute or to determine which team goes first, since it is considered to be a completely fair method that is based purely on luck.

10.   **TWO CENTS' WORTH** – It is speculated that originally a gambling card player had to pay two cents in order to join the game. It has been used for some time to refer to a value being attached to someone's views. If a person is going to give their opinion on something, they may say that they'll give their "two cents' worth."

A Penny in My Pocket
Discussion Questions

Chapters 1-2

1. How did Jay's social studies project affect his relationship with his brother and sister? Can you think of a time when something like that has happened in your family?
2. Name some ways a new immigrant might try to fit into a new country.
3. Why do you think Chapter Three is called "A Penny Saved is a Penny Earned?"
4. What were the similarities between Raj in Chapter One and Alex in Chapter Two?
5. Have you ever felt pressured to do something you knew was wrong? How did you deal with it? Think of some different ways to deal with negative peer pressure.

Chapters 3-4

1. Amelia compared her friendship with Katherine to that of Lucy and Ethel from *I Love Lucy*. Penny could relate to Jo in *Little Women*. Name a character from a book, movie or television show to whom you can relate and explain your choice.
2. Why was the war called The Great War and not World War I, like it is referred to today?
3. Do you think it would be hard to follow food restrictions? Why or why not?
4. The sounds of church bells and fire engine sirens during Penny's sleep caused her to dream that firemen were on their way to church. Have you ever worked something into a dream like that?

Chapters 5-6
1. Michael was hoping to play a solo of the song, "Take the 'A' Train" in the band concert. Listen to some music by Duke Ellington and describe how it makes you feel.
2. Chapter Five is called "In for a Penny, In for a Pound." Read the idiom glossary at the end of the book to find out what that expression means. Why do you think it was chosen as the name of the chapter?
3. Michael kept wearing the same lucky shirt. Do you ever wear or carry something lucky? If so, what and why?
4. Joseph bought himself a harmonica. What would you buy with your first paycheck?
5. Why wouldn't any of the employees at *The Amsterdam News* have been allowed into The Cotton Club?
6. Joseph wanted to see two specific baseball players play against each other. Would that have ever happened back then? Why or why not?

Chapters 7-8
1. Maggie went into detail describing her favorite food. Can you describe your favorite food in a way that would make someone else hungry?
2. Have you ever had to memorize lines? Did you use a certain method to memorize them? If so, what was it? Try and memorize Maggie's monologue from *A Midsummer Night's Dream*.
3. How would you and your family have to change your lifestyle if someone in your family lost a job? Do you think you could do it?
4. Have you ever run a sidewalk business such as a lemonade stand? What type of business was it?

Think about the reasons it was or wasn't successful.
5. Do you have any other ideas for a business? What are they?
6. Do some research to find out what protections were put in place to keep people's investments in banks and the stock market safer (see the book's website for some helpful links).

Chapters 9-10
1. Do you remember the attacks on New York and Washington on September 11, 2001 or do you know about them through TV, newspapers and magazines?
2. What are your feelings when you see it talked about on its anniversary every year?
3. Do you think news programs should still talk about and show the images of the attacks?
4. If you were allowed to make a telephone call to the President of the United States to give your opinion on how we should be handling terrorism, what would you say?
5. Think of something you might say to a soldier if you saw one in the airport or elsewhere.
6. Think of something you might do to help a soldier overseas or his family at home. Then do it! The website has a link for this.

Chapter 11 and general discussion questions
1. Were you surprised by some of the relationships that were shown between the students and the children from the years of the old pennies? In what way?
2. Did you have a favorite character in the book? If so, who was it and why?

3. Did you or your parents immigrate to this country? What was the experience like for you and/or them?
4. Do you know any recent immigrants to the United States? What could you do to make their adjustment more comfortable?
5. What is the difference between legal and illegal immigration?
6. Do you think you would be able to adjust to living in a different country, especially one that speaks a different language?
7. Have you ever traveled to another country where they spoke a different language? What did that feel like?
8. Would you ever want to live in another country? If so, which one and why?
9. If you see a penny, do you pick it up?

Author's Note:

The seed for this book was planted several years ago, when I found a 1918 penny. I couldn't believe what an old penny I'd found and I just held it, imagining all of its travels through the years. I set the penny in a prominent place, as a reminder that one day I really should write a book about it. During the course of a household move, the penny was put in a "safe" place, never to be found again. I finally did write the book and later realized I had subconsciously given Penny's 1918 penny in Chapter Four a similar fate as my penny.

In the front of the book, I have included the required legal wording that all characters, incidents, etc. are fictitious. I do want to emphasize that painstaking effort went into making sure that dates, times, and actual historic incidents are accurately represented. When a historical event, date or time is referenced, you can trust that it is based on documented historical facts. This book is intended to be used as a way to learn accurate historical facts in a fictional setting. A complete bibliography is available from the publisher upon request.

Please visit the website: apennyinmypocket.com for activities and interesting links relating to the book.

About the author:

Joyce Hill lives outside of Atlanta with her husband, a son and daughter, two dogs and three cats. She's a graduate of Wake Forest University with degrees in Business Administration and Sociology. Her many former lives include being an internal auditor, a commercial banker, and an activities coordinator for seniors. She has lived up and down the East Coast, and in Canada. Her hobbies include reading, walking and traveling.

CPSIA information can be obtained at www.ICGtesting.com
227815LV00001B/29/P

9 780979 581816